Longbourn's Lark: A Pride and Prejudice Variation

A Convenient Marriage, Volume 1

Meg Osborne

Published by Meg Osborne, 2020.

LONGBOURN'S LARK: A PRIDE AND PREJUDICE VARIATION

First edition. March 31, 2020.

Copyright © 2020 Meg Osborne.

ISBN: 978-1393469605

Written by Meg Osborne.

Chapter One

M ary Bennet slid into her familiar and favourite seat, in front of the pianoforte she thought of as hers and ran her fingers lightly over the keys. The usual chaos that echoed throughout Longbourn was quieted due, in part, to the absence of Lydia and Kitty, who had insisted on walking to Meryton to pay a visit to the regiment, undaunted by the promise of rain and determined only in succeeding in their mission. They had even invited her, Mary, to accompany them, which invitation she had primly refused. Their flirtations were shocking to quiet, shy Mary, and yet neither of her young sisters seemed in the slightest bit embarrassed to be observed acting so free and friendly with the laughing young men that made up the Meryton regiment.

Mary began to pick out a tune that she had heard at the recent assembly, wishing she had been brave enough to enquire of the musicians the name of the piece. She had intended to, hovering as close as she dared so that she might catch a glimpse of their sheet music, or draw someone into some conversation, perhaps be invited to play something herself. Her eyes fluttered closed as she indulged in the happy daydream for half a moment. She would play, and everyone would admire her talent, praise her for her skill, and at last, she would be the

Bennet daughter that everyone acknowledged. She hit a wrong note, and in frustration pounded out a discordant end to the piece. It had not happened, of course. It never did. She might as well be invisible, for all the notice anyone paid her. Even her sisters scarcely acknowledged her presence. Jane was too busy with this new Mr Bingley to pay any mind to her own family, and Mary was only too glad to stay out of Elizabeth's notice. She frowned. Her sister had a sharp tongue and was eager to use it on her, whenever Mary said a word that did not meet with her approval.

Slowly, her frown gave way to a smile. Today, all her sisters were out, or busy. The house was quiet, and she was free to play as much as she chose without fear of censure. Hovering over another chord, she leaned into it, her confidence growing as she played, and her fingers flying over the familiar notes as she traced out an old favourite of hers, a piece she could play in her sleep. *There!* she thought, hitting the last notes with a flourish. *That has cleared some cobwebs away.* She played another piece, and then another, gaining confidence in her playing and finding enjoyment at being allowed to do as she wished without offending her family's ears.

Minutes passed without Mary's notice, for if she heard the large clock on the mantel chime the hour, she did not pay it any heed, so lost was she in her music. She began to find herself humming along a melody to her own accompaniment and then felt brave enough to sing the words to a particularly pretty song she had long favoured. She sang rarely around her family, although she loved to do it, because singing before company made her nervous, and her nerves, in turn, made her voice wander from true, and the whole effect was mortifying for one who truly adored music as much as she did. Here, unheard and unobserved, she might sing and play to her heart's content, and she did so, her voice soaring in pitch and volume. She halted only at the sound of an unfamiliar gentleman's cough, and she leapt back from the piano as if it had burnt her.

"Oh, please forgive me!" the offending gentleman said. "I did not mean to frighten you."

"Frighten me?" Mary yelped, breathing hard. "I - I -" She glanced around in desperation. Who was this stranger, and what was he doing in the parlour of Longbourn?

"Your housekeeper showed me through - she did introduce me, and I felt sure you had heard us, but -"

The gentleman was tall and dressed elegantly enough, Mary presumed, although she knew little enough of fashion to make any real judgment. There was some familiarity to his face and she wondered fleetingly if they had met before. Then, fearful of being caught staring, she dropped her gaze.

"You have come to see my father, I suppose," she said. "He is in his study, I shall fetch him."

"No," the gentleman said, with a nervous laugh.

"One of my sisters, then? I am afraid you will be disappointed, for they are all out at present, but -"

"No, you misunderstand me, Miss - uh -" He hesitated, flushing a warm red as he struggled to recall the name she had not yet given him.

"Bennet," Mary said, quietly. "Mary Bennet."

"Miss Bennet." The gentleman smiled, warmly, at her, ducking his gaze slightly to meet hers. "I am Colonel Fitzwilliam. I am in search of a cousin of mine who is staying near here, and I'm afraid I lost my way. Your house was the first

I came to, and I stopped in only to ask for directions. I must ask your forgiveness for disturbing you, and for upsetting you by my presence. I bid the housekeeper not to disturb anyone, but -"

"Mary?" Mr Bennet's thundering voice came down the corridor. "Jennings tells me there is a gentleman here to see me, but -"

Colonel Fitzwilliam straightened and turned his attention to the doorway as Mr Bennet stomped through it.

"I am he, sir," he said, bowing slightly in greeting. "Please forgive me for disturbing your peace, and that of your daughter."

"Oh, never mind Mary!" Mr Bennet said, dismissing his apology with the wave of his hand. He squinted at their visitor. "How can I help you, Mr -"

"Colonel," Mary supplied, shrinking back once more as both gentlemen's gazes swivelled towards her. "Colonel Fitzwilliam," she whispered.

"Colonel?" Mr Bennet blinked, turning back to their visitor with renewed interest. "Well, indeed. And what brings you to Longbourn, Colonel Fitzwilliam?"

COLONEL RICHARD FITZWILLIAM gratefully accepted the tea that was offered to him, for he felt as if he had been walking for hours in the Hertfordshire countryside, and spent weeks on his feet before that with his regiment. The comforts of home were a distant memory to him, and he thought Longbourn a very comfortable home indeed.

"If it is Mr Darcy you seek then you've not got far to go," Mr Bennet said, his words muffled by the large mouthful of fruitcake he was working on. "It's three or four miles in that direction." He waved his hand towards the window. "But you might as well stay here and rest a quarter hour before moving on. You're cousins, did you say?"

"That's right," Colonel Fitzwilliam clarified. He glanced towards the piano, which the young Miss Bennet - Mary, he thought her name was - had hurried away from the instant he was invited to stay by her father. Instead, she sat primly on a chair opposite them, watching their conversation intently, but offering nothing by way of contribution. Richard felt a flash of guilt for disturbing her and stumbling upon them so suddenly. He could only imagine the flash of fear she must have felt to look up and see him - a stranger - standing before her in that very room, without warning or escort. It had not been his intention to blunder into a stranger's house and frighten his daughter, of course. In fact, Richard had not intended on entering at all, but his query of whether the gentleman of the house was at home was taken for a request to see him, and the housekeeper had obediently hurried him into the parlour, and now they were happily taking tea as if they were old friends and not new acquaintances.

"You do not look a bit alike!" Mr Bennet remarked, taking a loud gulp of his tea. "Still I suppose that might be taken as a compliment to one of you."

Richard smiled, vaguely, but was not sure whether Mr Bennet intended his comment as a joke or an insult.

"You'll be well acquainted with Mr Bingley as well, then?" Mr Bennet prompted. "He seems a fine enough fellow, and being head of a house full of young ladies I certainly hear more than I need to about the man." His eyes twinkled. "You must count yourself fortunate, Colonel, not to call at Longbourn while my wife is at home, I do not doubt she would endeavour to trap you here until you pledged to marry at least one of our daughters." He chuckled. "Is that not so, Mary?"

Mary said nothing, but when Richard glanced up at her, he saw her eyes flash with anger or embarrassment, he was not sure which.

"I have only met Mr Bingley once, some years ago," Richard said, eager to return Mr Bennet to an altogether safer topic of conversation and spare his daughter whatever anxiety this last comment had provoked. "And his sister, not at all, although I am of course obliged to them for their hospitality."

"Do you intend on staying long in Hertfordshire, Colonel Fitzwilliam?"

It took Richard a moment to realise that he had not imagined the question but that Mary Bennet herself had asked it. When he glanced at her, her gaze was fixed once more on the tea-tray, so that she might have appeared to have made the enquiry of the room at large, were it not for her use of his name.

"Not long, no. I am on my way to Kent." He grimaced, almost without meaning to. Kent meant Rosings, which meant Aunt Catherine. He called to visit Darcy first as a precursor to that, and for the chance to seek the advice of his cousin on how best to manage their shared aunt. It was Aunt Catherine's request that had him travel at all, for he had been half of a mind to go north, until her summons had arrived. She wished to ascertain for herself that he was not too badly off after the war. There had been some rumour of his taking ill, or suffering an injury, and whilst it would be indelicate to inquire of the nature of his illness, she wished to see her "dear nephew" for herself and be assured of his well-being. Richard had smirked. He was not sure he was ever her "dear" nephew when Darcy was also in consideration. Her "other" nephew, perhaps. War had apparently raised him in her estimation, but he was not one to jettison family responsibilities and was obliged to call on her. Kent would make a pleasant change of pace, and, fortified after a brief stint in Hertfordshire, Richard thought he would manage the winter very well.

"Ah, then it is indeed a pity our house is so quiet, for we have another guest staying here who hails *from* Kent!" Mr Bennet returned his teacup to its saucer with a musical clink. "My cousin, Mr Collins is a curate there."

"I believe," Marys' voice came, quietly, from her corner once more. "I believe his patroness is aunt to Mr Darcy, a Lady Catherine de Bourgh."

This prompted even Mr Bennet to look shrewdly at his daughter.

"You listen to his tales with more patience than I do, Mary!" To Richard: "Are you acquainted with this Lady Catherine de Bourgh?"

"A little," Richard admitted with a smile. "She is my aunt also."

"Then you had better be on your way sooner rather than later," Mr Bennet remarked. "For Mr Collins shall never wish to release you once he learns of your relationship. He has already attempted to align himself quite closely with Mr Darcy, with, ah, limited success."

"Indeed!" Richard could not help but laugh at the image this short description conjured up. He could well imagine Darcy trying to evade a growing friendship with any man so linked with Lady Catherine, and the notion that that man appeared eager for friendship would only serve to push Darcy further into retreat. "How fortunate that I should come at such a time!" Richard remarked. "And how providential that I should make your acquaintance first!"

Chapter Two

"Well, Miss Bingley, Mr Bingley, I must congratulate you on securing such a fine, elegant property." Mr Collins clapped his hands and beamed benevolently at their friends as if he were bestowing a great compliment, which was nonetheless undone by his next words. "It does not compare entirely unfavourably with Rosings, would not you say, Mr Darcy?"

Elizabeth rolled her eyes skywards, but was nonetheless amused to see Darcy mutter something in agreement and turn away almost immediately to engage Mrs Bennet in conversation. The fact that poor Mr Darcy chose her mother as a preferable companion to her cousin made Elizabeth bite her tongue hard to keep from laughing out loud. Unfortunately, she must have made some sound, however slight, for Mr Collins turned his attention directly to her.

"I do not say it compares exactly, my dear cousin Elizabeth, because, of course, Rosings is far superior in its style and position, as is entirely befitting for one of Lady Catherine de Bourgh's standing..."

Elizabeth plastered a polite smile on her face, and allowed her thoughts to wander, ensuring only that she nodded at intermittent moments to give the impression of listening to all that Mr Collins chose to say. She was fortunate, having two sisters who twittered just as happily about topics she had no interest in, that she had perfected this skill of appearing to pay attention whilst indulging in her own thoughts quite some time previously. It was a talent that continued to serve her well.

The small party that had intended on calling on Netherfield had doubled, for when Jane and Elizabeth mentioned making the journey on foot, Mr Collins had jumped up and offered to escort them, as he was very eager to form a better acquaintance with Mr Darcy on account of Lady Catherine. This had been disappointing, but Elizabeth did not anticipate Mr Collins' presence to be unduly detrimental to her true intent on calling: that it might afford Jane and Mr Bingley a better opportunity to converse than they had had at Meryton. Mr Collin's suggestion had somehow sparked Mrs Bennet's interest, and she, too, insisted on accompanying her daughters to call on "dear Mr Bingley". Elizabeth did not doubt her mother's intention was similar to her own but did rather suspect that her methods would be lacking in tact and serve to do more harm than good in furthering the fragile connection between Jane and Mr Bingley. Still, Mrs Bennet would not be dissuaded, and eventually all four made the short journey from Longbourn to Netherfield by carriage.

"Miss Eliza, I am surprised that only you and dearest Jane came to visit us. When I saw your cousin and mother in the carriage with you, I half expected all of your sisters to be within, as well." Caroline Bingley's comment was made with every impression of politeness but there was no mistaking her critical tone.

"It is rather a small carriage to comfortably seat such a party. In any case, Mary wished to remain at home, and Lydia and Kitty had...other plans." Lizzy felt a flash of hesitation before admitting her younger sisters' enthusiasm had been for Meryton and for the regiment, sure that saying so would merely give Caroline Bingley more ammunition with which to make thinly veiled criticisms of their family, which Lizzy did not wish to reach Mr Bingley's ears. He seemed a charming man, and perfectly content to know their family and consider them friends, but his sister's opinion of them had never been concealed and Lizzy feared that this, combined with Mr Darcy's evident disdain for her and her whole family would serve to discourage Mr Bingley from pursuing any match with Jane. Lizzy's sole intention was to see her sister happily married, and although she believed in her heart there was no man truly good enough to be worthy of Jane's affections, Mr Bingley appeared to have won them, and as he was quite the nicest gentleman of their acquaintance, he would have to do. They would marry, Elizabeth was determined.

"Oh, yes! My two younger daughters, you know, Mr Darcy, Catherine and Lydia, do you remember them from the Meryton assembly? Such happy, jolly creatures!"

Mr Darcy intimated that he did, and Lizzy found herself watching him so closely that she could hardly miss the brief flash of irritation that crossed his features at the memory of her sisters. Lizzy bristled in annoyance. It was one thing for her to admit privately that Lydia and Kitty could be rowdy and unladylike, but to see Mr Darcy silently possessing such an opinion merely made him still more obnoxious in her estimation.

"Well, they were determined to walk all the way to Meryton and visit the regiment! Is that not a jolly occupation for them?"

"I wonder that you are so fond of them spending time with such people, Mrs Bennet," Caroline's voice was smooth, but Lizzy could detect the danger. Mrs Bennet was less perceptive and laughed off any suggestion of impropriety.

"On the contrary, I envy them their youth and vitality!" She laughed. "I do think the soldiers such amiable, handsome young men. Do not you agree, Mr Darcy?"

"Not all soldiers," Darcy grumbled. He cleared his throat, glancing up and noticing Elizabeth's eyes on his. "That is, I cannot speak of all soldiers. Those I am acquainted with I consider to be fine, upstanding men."

"That's right!" Caroline trilled. "Your cousin is a colonel, is not he?" She turned a triumphant smile towards Elizabeth. "Colonel Fitzwilliam is due to stay with us a few days this week. When did he say he was to arrive, Mr Darcy?"

"Soon," Mr Darcy said, vaguely. "Charles, I wonder if I might ask a question about one of your horses. I noticed it limping a little last time we went out and it occurs to me that perhaps it has a touch of laminitis..."

Charles, unhappily taken away from the quiet conversation he had been having with Jane, turned a pained look towards his friend.

"You had better take it up with Hodges, in that case, Darcy. You know I am hardly an expert in horses. I can ride 'em and appreciate 'em as well as any other gentleman but beyond that...!" he shrugged, comically, and the party laughed.

Jane has done well to find such a happy, well-meaning gentleman to fall in love with, Lizzy thought, watching the pair return to their conversation with a soft smile. A sharp sigh from Mr Darcy drew her attention, and she noticed he did not regard the couple with anything matching her affection. His perpetual scowl was back in place, with such ferocity that Lizzy almost laughed to see it, for he did look such a comical version of himself. *What a pity Mr Bingley's friend has not one-tenth of his amiability,* she thought, with a wistful sigh of her own. Certainly, Mr Darcy offered much to be admired. He was handsome, and wealthy, and utterly too aware of the fact, and of his position in society relative to others. Lizzy lifted her chin. She had never admired pride in a person, and Mr Darcy possessed it in spades.

Well, it is not for my own sake or Mr Darcy's that I am here, she reminded herself. *I wish only to see dear Jane happy, and if Mr Bingley is the man who will make her so, then I will bear whoever he happens to surround himself with.* His sister Caroline might be unavoidable, but Lizzy could not help but wish he had better taste in friends than Mr Darcy.

As if her thoughts had taken wings, Mr Darcy looked up at this moment, meeting her eyes with his own, and looking away just as quickly. *Well, Lizzy,* she thought. *It seems the feeling is mutual: Mr Darcy is precisely as fond of you as you are of him. What a pity we must be forced into proximity because of the affection we have for those who would choose one another!*

MR FITZWILLIAM DARCY propped his elbow on the corner of a table, and rested his chin on his hand, hoping to disguise his tiredness. He need not have worried over disguising it, for Mr Collins was oblivious to any discomfort in his companions, merely continuing on with his tale as if he were giving a sermon and not engaged in conversation.

Darcy's eyes travelled over his friends. Jane and Mr Bingley were sitting with every impression of rapt attention, although Darcy fancied they were rather more concerned with observing, whilst not appearing to observe, one another. Mrs Bennet dozed contentedly in a corner, making no sound apart from the occasional snore which went unremarked upon by anybody present. Caroline Bingley made no effort to conceal her dislike of Mr Collins, affecting a snide smile whenever he happened to glance in her direction, and trying, whenever he paused for breath, to interrupt and recapture the conversation for her own ends. Mr Collins, for his part, was oblivious to her attempts and continued talking as if she had made no sound. Only Elizabeth Bennet seemed to share Darcy's predicament. She was, like her sister, giving an impression of rapt attention, but Darcy could tell from the way her eyes strayed first to the bookshelves, and then to the window, that her mind was actively seeking alternative engagement. Their eyes met, momentarily, and where Darcy hurried to glance away again, he got the impression that Elizabeth herself was prompted to laugh. She made a curious sound, disguised it as a cough, and when Mr Collins paused in his sermonizing to enquire after her health, assured him that she was "very well, thank you, only wondering if her cousin would be very much offended if she took a turn about the garden, in order to get some fresh air." This request was leapt upon by Mr Bingley, who offered to escort both Miss Bennets on a tour of the property, and it was soon decided that the whole party would take a turn about the gardens, much to Caroline Bingley's muttered irritation.

"I would much rather they take a turn about the property in the direction of Longbourn," she whispered, close enough to Darcy that he would be the only one to hear it. "What on earth do they mean, bringing that wretched man here?"

"I do not believe they had a great deal of choice," Darcy remarked, drily.

"In any case, I don't doubt he was almost as eager to see you as Miss Eliza was," Caroline said, with a sly smile. Darcy tried to ignore her. She had made three such mentions of Elizabeth Bennet in the past few days, ever since his innocent comment about her eyes had been taken entirely out of context. He might admire a woman for her appearance without pledging himself heart and soul to her, yet Caroline Bingley appeared to take the comment as a personal slight and was still exacting revenge upon him for it. And upon poor, unsuspecting Elizabeth, who had borne the brunt of Caroline's sarcasm to her face, and criticism behind her back.

"It is hardly my fault that Mr Collins views me as a link to my aunt," he said, deciding not to acknowledge Caroline's comments about Elizabeth at all, and confine his response solely to Mr Collins and Lady Catherine de Bourgh. "She is his patroness, and he is apparently eager to please her."

Caroline said nothing, but sniffed.

"Well, of course, I am sure Lady Catherine is well worthy of his esteem, only -" Darcy did not listen any longer, for Charles let out a shout that caught his attention.

"I say, Darcy, look who comes up the driveway! Is that not your cousin?"

Darcy looked, and sure enough he detected the tall, broad-shouldered figure of Colonel Richard Fitzwilliam.

"Good man!" he cried, shrugging off Caroline's company, and striding forward to welcome his cousin with a hearty embrace. "I did not expect you so soon! Did you ride all the way from London?"

"Almost," Richard said, with an unreadable grin. "Only a slight detour once I reached Hertfordshire." He glanced past Darcy to where Charles and Caroline stood with Mrs Bennet, Jane, Elizabeth and Mr Collins. "Now I must make my greatest thanks to Mr and Miss Bingley for allowing a wayward soldier to join their ranks for a few days." He bowed low, which made Charles laugh with embarrassment, and Caroline nod, regally, as if such deference were the very least she expected from a visiting guest of Mr Darcy's, and one who had made his career in the army, rather than standing to inherit, as Darcy did. He was embarrassed on her behalf, but his cousin was such a good sort he doubted Richard would take any offence from such a haughty acknowledgement.

"These are our neighbours, Colonel Fitzwilliam," Mr Bingley said, remembering his role as host. "Mrs Bennet, Miss Jane and Miss Elizabeth Bennet, and their cousin Mr Collins, from -"

"Longbourn?" Richard offered, his eyes twinkling.

Everyone glanced at him in surprise, and he permitted himself a moment of laughter, before offering his explanation.

"Forgive me, I could not help but tease. I have come directly from Longbourn myself. You see, despite my cousin's faultless directions, it appears I left my navigational brains behind me with my uniform. In short: I lost my way, and stumbled upon a fine looking house, where I stopped to enquire of the way to Netherfield. This house was called Longbourn, and a very kind gentleman - your father - directed me here with all welcome and goodwill. I am delighted to meet his wife, two more of his daughters, and his cousin, in such fine company."

"Two more?" Caroline asked, with unmistakable interest. Her ear for gossip was surely burning, for she arched an eyebrow and leaned closer in order that she might press Colonel Fitzwilliam for details. "Which of the others did you meet already?"

"A Miss Mary Bennet," Colonel Fitzwilliam said, with a brief smile towards Elizabeth and Jane. "She is musical, I believe, or rather, she would be, were it not for uncultured oafs such as myself disturbing her peace and practice by clattering in unannounced." He laughed, as if remembering some funny adventure that nobody else present was privy to.

"Well!" Mrs Bennet breathed, pushing herself forward as if she had determined to know this new arrival better. "I am very pleased to hear that you have already met my husband, Mr -"

"Colonel," Darcy replied automatically.

"Colonel Fitzwilliam." Mrs Bennet beamed at him, but even Darcy could see the wheels turning in her head. Another eligible bachelor, and one already acquainted with half her family...

"Come, Richard, no doubt you are tired and eager to rest after your journey," Darcy said, eager to save his cousin from the same fate he and his friend had already suffered. "Even if you came by way of Longbourn it would have been a walk for you. Let's go inside and we might speak for a moment or two while the party finishes their walk."

He escorted his cousin indoors before anybody - in particular Mrs Bennet or Caroline Bingley - could protest the idea.

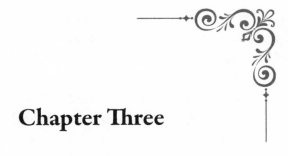

Chapter Three

"It is good to see you, cousin!" Richard said, as he and Darcy were seated in a small study, both armed with brandies, and the door closed against the outside world. Darcy had ushered him into the small room, forgoing the parlour almost entirely. Had it been any other person but Darcy, Richard might have made some question about a surprising desire for privacy, but he knew his cousin well and felt certain this was to guard against the rest of their party hurrying back to join them too soon.

"And I, you! I half feared you still suffering, from the contents of your last letter," Darcy commented.

"Only for such vivacious company as yours, William." Richard saluted him with his brandy glass, and grinned toothily at the scowl his cousin sent in his direction. "You see? In London, I am greeted with smiles and good-humour. I have to come all the way out to the Hertfordshire countryside for a true Fitzwilliam Darcy welcome."

"Indeed," Darcy grumbled, fixing his gaze on the contents of his glass, and watching the surface of the amber liquid ripple and reflect the light.

"No, in all honesty, I needed the fortification of your company before I press on to Kent." Richard grimaced. "Aunt Catherine has invited me to visit -"

"Invited?"

"Commanded." Richard amended. "There was little option of my refusing. I could delay her only, and she was content enough to hear I would be stopping to visit you." He took a sip of his drink. "I rather think she intends me to convince you to come on to Rosings with me, so that we might all be together for Christmas." He grinned. "What a happy occasion that might be!"

Darcy snorted, and Richard returned to his drink. He knew his cousin felt as uncomfortable as he did at Rosings - if not less so. Aunt Catherine had been fixing to match Darcy and her daughter Anne since the two were babies, and with every year that passed her hints became less and less nuanced. Poor Darcy had no interest in his cousin, beyond what was proper as his relation and friend, and Anne, too, had no love for Darcy, although Richard knew that she valued his friendship. It made for awkward conversation and even more awkward company, and he had often been forced to hone his good humour in an attempt to lighten the mood over a particularly dour dining table, or sitting around the piano.

"And how is Georgiana?" he asked, his memory of the piano sparking another memory of his cousin, Darcy's sister, who was the most musical of the family. "Is she not here with you?"

"No." Darcy looked shocked at the notion. "She is quite content, and busy with her studies, her music, her..." he waved his hand, as if to encapsulate the mysterious world inhabited by young ladies, and which their elder brothers took less than little interest in.

The cousins lapsed into companionable silence for a few moments, before Darcy cleared his throat and spoke again.

"You visited Longbourn on your way here?"

"I did," Richard smiled. "It was not my intention, but it seems providence had other ideas. Mr Bennet seems a good fellow."

Darcy snorted.

"Is not he?"

"He is perhaps the most sensible member of the family," Darcy conceded. "Except for -" he hesitated. "No, I wager him to be the most sensible, although he appears to be surrounded by enough women to make that count for little."

"How many daughters?" Richard grinned. "Four? No, five. I have met three now, I believe." He shrugged his shoulders. "And fine ladies they seem, too. It is clear your friend Charles is somewhat smitten with the fair one - what was her name, Jane?"

Darcy rolled his eyes skywards.

"Ah, you disapprove!" Richard laughed. "But of course. When has Fitzwilliam Darcy ever approved of true love?"

"I have no problem with true love," Darcy countered. "I question that this is anything other than opportunity and taking advantage of my friend's ability to develop affection at the first smile from a pretty face."

"Nothing wrong with a pretty face," Richard said, cheerfully, recalling a certain unusually striking face that might even be called such, when it was adorned with the smile that had only fleetingly been upon it when they met. "Provided it does not conceal an ugly character."

"When did you become a philosopher?" Darcy said, grumpily.

"Around the same time you became a misery, I expect." Richard stood, striding over to Charles' brandy decanter and pouring himself another healthy measure. "Come, William. There's nothing wrong with falling in love. We all wish to do it sometime, surely?" He glanced out of the corner of his eye at his cousin, and was gratified to see him shift uncomfortably in his seat. *Aha! So I have struck a nerve.* "Take you, for example,"

"Me, for example?" Darcy sighed, extravagantly. "What insights do our five minutes' reacquaintance afford you on the state of my heart?"

To any other man, Darcy's tone might have sounded entirely oppositional, and full of foreboding. To Richard, this was the same boy he had fought with and bantered with all his life. He would not be so easily deterred.

"You do not wish to marry our cousin, and so you avoid visiting Rosings, fearing Lady Catherine's less-than-subtle attempts to engineer it, when there remains an altogether easier solution."

"Yes?" Darcy lifted his gaze. "And what might that be, for surely you have puzzled out an answer and wish to deliver it as a missive from heaven. Come, cousin. How shall I avoid a marriage I do not wish, without offending the family I value?"

"Marry someone else." Richard uttered the phrase with the utmost simplicity and straightforwardness.

"So easy!" Darcy said, downing the last of his drink and returning his glass to the table top with a thump. "And who, pray, am I to marry?"

"Well," Richard leaned back against the bookshelves and folded his arms across his chest, eyeing his cousin with a merry expression upon his face. "There appears to be a house full of eligible young ladies just three miles yonder. Even discounting Jane - or perhaps one or two others that do not meet your particularly high standards, I can see that leaves you at least one other lady to choose from. Elizabeth Bennet, perhaps." He was watching his cousin carefully, and did not miss the tiny muscle that tensed in Darcy's jaw at the mention of this particular young lady. Understanding his cousin perhaps better than he did himself, however, he did not pursue the matter, reckoning it would serve him better to circle back to the suggestion at a later time. Sensing Darcy was growing weary of the discussion he determined to resolve it quickly, and humorously.

"Or, if not Elizabeth Bennet, then perhaps another lady closer to home." His eyes twinkled with humour. "I am quite sure Caroline Bingley would not be averse to any interest you might show her."

"WELL, HERE WE ARE, home again," Jane Bennet said, as she and Elizabeth crossed the threshold of Longbourn.

"Mary!" Elizabeth cried, spotting her sister in the corridor. "What on earth are you doing lurking in the shadows like that, you scared us half to death!"

"Did you have a pleasant visit to Netherfield?" Mary asked, directing her question to Jane, rather than Elizabeth, in hopes it might be answered without criticism.

"What do you care?" Elizabeth asked, lazily. "I thought you had "no interest in visiting people we are scarcely acquainted with".

Mary frowned at having her own words thrown back at her. Had she really been so dismissive of Jane and Elisabeth's plans when they had volunteered them at the breakfast table?

"You are sweet to ask, Mary," Jane said, as the three girls walked into the parlour. "Yes, we had a very nice time. Mr Bingley sends his regards, as do his sister and Mr Darcy, of course."

"And Colonel Fitzwilliam!" Elizabeth put in, as she claimed the sofa for her own, and stretched out on it. "It appears you made quite an impression on the newest arrival to Hertfordshire!"

Mary's cheeks flushed, and she struggled to keep an instinctive smile from her face, until she looked up at her sisters in time to catch a glance exchanged between Jane and Elizabeth. Her heart sank. Elizabeth was teasing her, clearly. Colonel Fitzwilliam had not mentioned her at all. And why should he? They met but by chance, and spoke for scarcely half an hour. Colonel Fitzwilliam's attention had almost entirely been taken up with Mr Bennet, and Mary was but an afterthought. *As usual.*

"How strange that he should be cousin to Mr Darcy!" Elizabeth remarked, with a laugh. "For I am sure I never came across two more dissimilar gentlemen!" She paused. "Except, perhaps, for Mr Darcy and Mr *Bingley.*" This was accompanied with a pointed glance towards Jane, which Mary scarcely noticed.

"I thought them quite alike, actually!" she remarked. "For they were both tall and had such dark hair, although I grant you Colonel Fitzwilliam smiles a good deal more than Mr Darcy, but -" Mary stopped speaking, all of a sudden aware of the silence that had fallen over both her sisters while she made her observations. "I mean, I had scarcely a quarter hour upon which to make any judgment at all," she said, flustered. "And I am sure seeing them standing next to one another would lead me to an entirely different conclusion."

Rather than resolving the matter, this further comment seemed to provoke her surprised sisters into smiles, and Mary braced herself for the joke at her expense she felt sure was coming.

"You are quite perceptive, Mary," Jane said, softly. "I am sure you are right. In fact, now that you mention it, I believe I recognised the same likeness in feature in both Mr Darcy and Colonel Fitzwilliam." She exchanged a wordless glance with Elizabeth. "Although I grant the latter far less serious than his cousin."

"Perhaps he might encourage Mr Darcy out of the scowl he so frequently wears!" Elizabeth remarked. "I cannot imagine what that gentleman has to be so ill-tempered about. He is wealthy and free do to just exactly as he pleases, and with such friendly companions as Mr Bingley and Colonel Fitzwilliam." She paused. "And Caroline Bingley. I suppose that is reason enough to scowl."

"Come, now, Elizabeth," Jane said, gently. "We only know of Mr Darcy what he shares, and that is little enough. We ought not to judge him too harshly."

Elizabeth opened her mouth to respond, but in the end accepted her sister's chiding with grace, and nodded.

"I suppose you are right, but I am predisposed not to think entirely well of the man after he snubbed me at Meryton," Elizabeth laughed, self-deprecatingly. "It is a lesson to me, that my own pride must be as strong as his, or I would not continue to be upset by it!"

Mary's ears pricked up. What snub? She had not been present for this, nor heard her sisters discussing it afterwards. Had Mr Darcy really upset her sister so deeply? She felt a flicker of sympathy for Elizabeth, for although they did not have a close relationship, she knew her sister often kept her true feelings hidden. It was, perhaps, their one trait in common. If Elizabeth had been upset, then Mary could well understand it. How often had she heard comments about her, muttered behind her back, and nursed them long after they had been forgotten by the one who spoke them?

"I am sure he did not mean it, Lizzy," Mary said, using the nickname for her sister that she rarely felt brave enough to use. "Whatever he said: he hardly knows you and can surely only be drawing a false conclusion, if he does not think highly of you already."

"Thank you, Mary," Elizabeth said, surprised and a little confused to receive such a compliment. The sisters fell into silence once more, but Mary felt as if a corner had been turned in their relationship, and there was the very beginning of understanding between them.

"Why don't you play for us, Mary?" Jane suggested, brightly. "Colonel Fitzwilliam was very taken by your musical abilities, did not he remark upon them to us at Netherfield Lizzy? Play whatever it was you were playing when he arrived, for I, at least, am eager to hear it!"

This was all the invitation Mary required, and she took her seat at the piano, taking a breath to steady her nerves as she played. She risked a glance at both of her sisters, expecting to see boredom or weary tolerance resting on their features. She was surprised, then, to notice pleasure and what might even have been affection on the faces of her two eldest sisters.

To think, she marvelled. *All this change wrought merely by Colonel Fitzwilliam's chance arrival. I do hope we might meet again. Who knows what else will happen under his influence?*

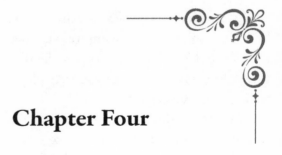

Chapter Four

"A ball?"

Darcy groaned, but he was apparently alone in deploring the plan, for every other person at the table remarked upon the fine plan Mr Bingley had suggested.

"It was not entirely my suggestion that I might take credit for it," he said, good-naturedly. "The youngest Bennet girl...what was her name...Lydia! She implored us to host some sort of get-together, and it seemed churlish to refuse." He beamed across the table at Richard. "Now, with your arrival, Colonel Fitzwilliam, it seems like the perfect excuse to host a small soiree." His glance reached Darcy's and fell a little. "It need not be a very large affair..."

"I do not imagine it will be!" Caroline Bingley asserted, with haughty indignance. "For who on earth shall we find to invite?"

"Come, Miss Bingley, surely there are at least half a dozen people in all of Hertfordshire who might meet your admirable standards and be found worthy of an invitation to a quiet evening among friends, here at Netherfield Park." Richard's tone was gently mocking, and Darcy lifted his eyes warningly to his cousin. He and Charles might be able to tolerate his cousin's good humour well enough, but Caroline Bingley was not renowned for her sense of humour, particularly when she was the cause of amusement. Her eyes flashed angrily and Richard, realising his danger, undid the comment with a deferential smile. "Of course, I know little of what I speak, for I have been so busy with the regiment I can scarily recall the last time I attend any such gathering, let alone considered the strain of hosting one. But it need not be an extravagant affair, surely? Perhaps just a meal, with a few close neighbours or friends for company."

This invited Bingley himself to weigh in, and utter the words that Darcy imagined his sister had most been dreading.

"We must have the Bennets, at the very least!"

Caroline sighed, but said nothing.

"The Bennets?" Mrs Hurst asked, from her corner of the table. She blinked, irritably, from her insistence on never wearing eyeglasses. "All of them?"

"Yes, all of them! We can hardly invite two sisters and not the other three, or exclude their parents."

"They will surely come, and fill half our table in doing so," Caroline observed. "And I must find another family with gentlemen to invite, or we shall be dreadfully ill-matched for dancing..."

Darcy groaned again. Why must "just a meal, with a few close neighbours" necessitate dancing?

"The middle Bennet daughter is very musical," Richard remarked, apropos of nothing. "So in inviting her, you might easily facilitate your entertainments as well."

Caroline pursed her lips, and glanced first at her brother and then him. Darcy felt certain she was waiting for either gentleman, or, preferably, both, to rally to her defence at this perceived slight from his cousin, and suggest that her own talents far exceeded those of Mary Bennet. Darcy was fond of music, and he missed hearing his sister Georgiana's skilful practice almost as much as he missed Georgiana herself. He had to admit, on the rare occasion he had had to hear Mary Bennet, that she certainly seemed fond of the piano, and played it with a spirit and feeling lacking in Caroline's perfunctory playing.

"You shall not wish to play all evening, Caroline," Bingley said, at last, skillfully managing his sister's threatened mood. "For then you would not be able to dance. Young Miss Mary is not fond of dancing, so why not let her play, and the rest of us dance, and then that will be a happy solution for all concerned.

"She does not dance?" Richard asked. When Darcy looked up at him surprised at this sudden and inexplicable interest in the, so far as he could tell, unremarkable Mary Bennet, his cousin's face was unreadable. "I felt sure all young ladies loved to dance," he remarked, with an easy shrug. "But then what knowledge have I of young ladies?" His eyes twinkled with amusement, but Darcy continued to stare at him for some moments, sure there was more to his cousin's comments than he could discern at present.

"Well it will not be much of a party if it is merely us six and a gaggle of Bennets," Caroline said, putting a sly emphasis on the word "gaggle" which provoked a snicker of laughter from Mrs Hurst. "Perhaps I will invite Mr Wainwright." Caroline pursed her lips. "He is only a curate, but he will perhaps be a steadying influence on the more excitable Bennets."

"If you are inviting curates, Caroline, you had better extend an invitation to Mr Collins as well," Mr Bingley said, with a generous smile.

Darcy felt another groan rise up in the back of his throat but checked it. There would be no escaping Mr Collins, for they could not very well exclude the man from an invitation extended to the rest of his family. At least this time Darcy would not face him alone: Colonel Fitzwilliam, as another nephew of his patroness Lady Catherine would draw at least equal attention.

"Yes, Mr Collins," Caroline turned a syrupy smile towards his cousin, and Darcy thought that she had not been so quick to forgive Colonel Fitzwilliam's perceived slight as she had appeared. "You have not met him properly yet, have you, Colonel?"

"I have not yet had the pleasure. Darcy quite spirited me away upon my arrival, although I did spy him standing next to Charles."

"I am sure he will be most eager to make your acquaintance, as he has been of Mr Darcy."

Colonel Fitzwilliam smiled back, oblivious to Caroline's implication, which was only too clear to the rest of the table.

"Well, Caroline," Bingley said, hurrying to change the subject and prevent his sister from being openly unkind about one of their guests. "When do you intend on hosting this small soiree? We ought to give more than a day's notice, I do not doubt..."

"KITTY! GIVE ME THAT back! Mama! Make her stop, it's so unfair, I-"

The squabbling between her two youngest sisters was interspersed with a weary shout from Mrs Bennet, and the sound of feet thundering over floorboards, slamming doors behind them. With a sigh, Lizzy glanced towards her own bedroom door, wondering if it was about to fly open and admit some unwelcome guest. Returning her attention to her book, she turned a page, but could not bring herself to read any more. Closing it, she laid it aside, flinging herself back on the bed in frustration. She had hardly been able to settle to her reading all day, having spent half the morning out walking, with the promise of a quiet afternoon with her newest acquisition.

"Mary, get out of the way! Why are you lurking in the corridor?" Kitty's shrill voice broke through Elizabeth's thoughts, and she sat up, crossing the room and sliding the door open just in time to see Mary slink back into her own room.

Closing the door quietly, Lizzy retraced her steps.

Of all her sisters, she was quite sure she understood Mary the least. They had never been close, and lately Mary had become increasingly irritating, always quoting from Fordyce or some such, or banging away on the piano when all anybody wanted was peace. She was at least generally quieter and more peaceful than either Lydia or Kitty alone, and doubly so when they were together. But Lizzy felt certain there was more to Mary than she had yet acknowledged. She saw it in the flash of light that appeared in Mary's grey eyes from time to time, or the smile that crept over her features when she was playing the piano unmolested and unaware of her audience.

She has absolutely no sense of humour, though! Lizzy thought, remembering the occasional teasing comment she had shot her sister's way which had been taken for insult and resulted in Mary stomping away and slamming a door. Elizabeth smiled, but it was not an entirely happy one. If Mary took all of Lizzy's words for slights, no wonder she was reluctant to open up to her, and no wonder they were basically strangers, despite living in the same house all their lives.

Feeling suddenly convicted of the way she had acted towards her sister before now, and wondering if it was misunderstanding, rather than some inherent dislike, that had kept them from becoming friends, Lizzy decided she would make one more attempt to bridge the gap of several years. She stood and made for the door, propelling herself into action before she changed her mind.

She knocked on Mary's bedroom door, and waited patiently until she heard her sister's hesitant voice.

"Who is it?"

"Only me!" Lizzy said, cheerfully pushing the door open and striding in. Seeing her sister was sitting upright in a chair, with the wretched but familiar Fordyce closed in her lap, Lizzy took a seat on her bed. "What are you doing?" She nodded towards the closed book. "Reading?"

"Oh," Mary glanced down, colouring slightly. "No. I was going to, but..."

She slid her hands around the book, and picked it up, glancing at it with something that might have been disdain, before laying it down on an end-table with a sigh. "Do you promise not to judge me terribly?"

This surprised Elizabeth, and she sat forward, regarding her sister with interest.

"You are my sister, Mary, you will get no judgment from me," Elizabeth said, seriously. She folded her hands in her lap and waited, expectantly, to be shocked by Mary's serious revelation.

"I am growing rather tired of Fordyce's sermons." This was whispered, as if it were some great and terrible secret, and it shocked Elizabeth so much that she laughed, clapping a hand over her mouth and swallowing her reaction when she saw how Mary recoiled at her reaction.

"I am sorry Mary!" Lizzy said, hurrying to undo the damage. "Forgive me! I was expecting some dreadful confession, and here you speak of not liking Fordyce as if it were a thing to be lamented!" Lizzy crossed, and slid the book into her own hands, opening it at random, and darting a scornful glance over a few words. "I believe you are the only one of us to have ever read it from cover to cover, let alone read any part of it more than once." With derision, Lizzy closed the book and dropped it on Mary's bed with a thump. "Dry, dreary Fordyce! There are so many more interesting things you might read, dear."

This use of "dear" had clearly struck Mary, for she looked up at Lizzy as if she was not quite sure she recognised her.

"I'll tell you what, I have a small collection of books that you are welcome to choose from. In fact, I think I know a perfect novel you might find enjoyable." She leaned forward, waggling her eyebrows comically at her sister. "Though I must warn you, it is altogether more scandalous than Fordyce. There are -" she dropped her voice to a whisper. "Scrapes. Adventures. Moral lessons. And love!"

"Love?" Mary whispered, flushing slightly.

"Oh, it is a pretty little romance. You must not think badly of it."

"Oh, no!" Mary said. "I don't."

This brought Elizabeth up short, and she folded her arms, regarding her sister with interest.

"Do you think - do you think Jane and Mr Bingley will marry?" Mary asked, with an affection of calm disinterest that did not deceive her sister for a moment.

"I hope they might," Lizzy said, carefully. "For she cares for him and I venture to imagine he thinks highly of her."

"He must," Mary said, with a nod. "For Jane is so lovely how could he not?"

"My sentiments entirely!" Lizzy smiled.

"He danced with her often at Meryton, didn't he?" Mary continued. "And he always likes to speak to her when they are in company. Is that how you know he loves her?"

"I would not say I *know*," Lizzy said. "But he certainly seems to prefer her company to many others."

Mary nodded, frowning slightly as if she were busily processing something but not yet ready to share her thoughts were her sister.

"Come along, I want to show you this novel. I hope you will read it, and then we can talk about it!" Lizzy grinned. "For I have long despaired of sharing books with any other of my sisters and expecting any intelligent conversation afterwards." This small compliment took a moment to register with Mary, but when it did, she lifted her eyes to Elizabeth's with a shy smile.

"In that case, I shall begin it this afternoon!"

Chapter Five

"An invitation to Netherfield Park!" Mrs Bennet cried, snatching the note out of her husband's hand one breakfast time before Mr Bennet had even had a chance to finish reading it himself. "Girls! What do you think of this? We have all been asked - and bless me they even extend their invitation to you, Mr Collins! - to dine at Netherfield Park tomorrow evening."

As her sisters exchanged excited comments about the promised dinner, Mary's heart sank. She did not enjoy these sorts of gatherings, marginally preferring the large assemblies to a smaller, more intimate dinner. At least at an assembly she might find some quiet corner to hide in, where she could enjoy the music and watch the dancing without being observed herself. A meal at Netherfield would mean a lot of dull conversation and no chance of escape without being thought rude. She sighed.

"Dear me, Mary, did you not sleep well?" Mr Bennet asked.

Mary straightened, surprised that anybody had noticed her at all, particularly her father, who had been at the centre of an excitable discussion between his wife and his eldest daughters.

"I am quite well, Father, I just -"

"You are about as excited as the promise of an evening at Netherfield Park as I am, I wager." He winked at her, and Mary smiled. She felt a special kinship with her father. Mr Bennet might not value her quite as highly as he did Elizabeth, but he and Mary were both of a quieter disposition than many of their other family members, and often, when she found a quiet corner, she was forced to share it with her father, that they might both hide a while from their more gregarious family members.

"But Mary, Colonel Fitzwilliam will be there," Elizabeth said.

Mary's eyes snapped up, suspicious of some slight, but her sister's face was innocent of all teasing.

"I am sure he will be eager to see you again, after your chance meeting the other day," Elizabeth said, encouragingly.

In spite of herself, Mary flushed a deep, hot red, and it was this, more than Elizabeth's innocent comment, that drew the notice of her younger sisters, who seized upon her evident discomfort.

"Colonel Fitzwilliam?" Lydia cried. "And who is he, pray? Has Mary found herself a suitor?"

Mary tried not to acknowledge the exaggerated shock that such a thing might happen to *Mary* of all the sisters, for Lydia was cruel quite often without meaning to be.

"He is Mr Darcy's cousin," Jane offered. "He came to Hertfordshire lately, and found himself at our door, rather than Mr Bingley's, I believe," she explained. "When he reached Netherfield, he could do little but praise father's hospitality and Mary's talent at the piano."

Mary's heart sank once more. Of course, Colonel Fitzwilliam could not be interested in seeing *her*. He might appreciate her musical abilities - but then how discerning could a Colonel from a regiment hope to be about music? It might be that once he had an opportunity to hear other ladies play even that interest would plummet.

"He was a fine fellow," Mr Bennet remarked, returning heartily to his breakfast. "In fact, I approve of him rather more than his cousin. I anticipate he is likewise unmarried, thus I give any one of you leave to marry him." He waved his fork around the table at each daughter in turn, resting at length on Mary. "Except for Jane," he amended, after a stern glance from his wife. "Who, I believe, has another beau in mind."

"Mr Bennet!" his wife screeched. "Do not speak so! Nothing has been confirmed yet, and we must not jinx it by -"

"My dear Mrs Bennet, I cannot keep pace with all of these romantic developments. I am but one man. I shall trust that you and my daughters might manage their own affairs and will return to a state of blissful ignorance. Recall it was you who demanded I make our neighbours' acquaintance in the first place, and had I not been at home when poor Colonel Fitzwilliam stumbled upon us then he might still be wandering around the Hertfordshire countryside lost and alone and scarcely fit to court anyone."

"He does not court anyone," Mrs Bennet said, with exaggerated patina. "We are all merely friends. It is very friendly. There is a hope that, in time, Mr Bingley and Jane -" she held her hand up. "But let us not speak any more on the matter. This evening might change everything." She clutched the invitation to her breast as if it were a royal decree, and hurried out of the room. "Jane! Lizzy! Finish your meals and join me upstairs, we must take a look at your wardrobe and decide what you might wear tomorrow evening. It is of the utmost importance that you both look particularly pretty, for even though it is merely a dinner I do not see why that precludes one looking elegant..."

With his wife's departure, a semblance of sanity reigned over the breakfast table once more, and Mr Bennet remarked,

"I do not understand this excitement over what is surely just a dinner with our neighbours. There is certainly no such interest over a meal at Lucas Lodge."

"You forget, father," Elizabeth remarked, with a sly smile. "Lucas Lodge houses only daughters. If an eligible bachelor were to pitch up on their doorstep things might be entirely different!"

Mary felt a smile tug at the corners of her lips, as she met Elizabeth's eye.

"Come, Mary," Elizabeth said, spontaneously. "You can join us. If Jane and I must suffer through Mama's wardrobe schemes, you might as well. Besides, I found my old blue silk the other day when I was putting something away and it would look so well against your dark hair. You must try it on, for it should fit you without the need of very much alteration."

"I CONFESS THIS IS A sight I have missed!" Richard said, with a contented sigh. He and Darcy had taken two of the Netherfield horses out for a ride and were happily admiring the great swathe of Hertfordshire countryside that stretched out before them. "There is fine country around here."

"It is quite beautiful enough, I suppose," Darcy remarked.

"You do not approve?" Richard shot him a sly glance. *And why am I not surprised that my critical cousin can find something to remark upon even here?*

"I neither approve nor disapprove. It is the English countryside, and quite charming enough in its way."

"It is no Derbyshire, though."

To Richard's surprise Darcy laughed, and when he glanced over at him, a self-deprecating grin had lifted his dark features into something approaching a smile.

"You know me well, cousin. And it does me good to have my bad temper pointed out to me."

Richard lifted his eyebrows. It was not an apology, but it was perhaps the closest he had known Darcy to offer in at least a decade.

"How does Georgiana fare?" Richard had waited until they were quite alone before asking after his younger cousin again, unsure how much Darcy had shared with his friends of Georgiana's narrow escape from George Wickham and subsequent low spirits.

"She is well, I think," Darcy said, his frown returning. "I hope to see her in the new year when I return to Pemberley."

"What a shame she could not be persuaded to accompany you here, then I might take you both on to Kent with me."

Darcy grimaced.

"You just wish for more bodies to place in between you and Aunt Catherine," he said.

"True enough!" Richard laughed. "She shall quiz me on my plans for the future, now that I have left the regiment."

"And what are your plans for the future?" Darcy quipped. "Now that you have left the regiment?"

"Rest!" Richard said, with an extravagant yawn. "Honestly, I feel as if I have worked so hard for so long that I can scarcely think beyond a warm hearth and a good brandy."

"Neither of which you will be permitted to enjoy unaccented at Rosings," Darcy reminded him. "But you might have your fill of it here at Netherfield, although I confess their library leaves a little wanting in terms of choice."

"Ideally, I wish to set up a home of my own," Richard confessed, his voice lowering. He had not spoken yet of his desire to marry, to have a family, to anyone. In fact, he had scarcely allowed himself to acknowledge the desire, but being here in Hertfordshire, it became apparent to him how deeply he had missed country life, and how much he yearned for the simplicity of a comfortable home and a happy wife.

"A bachelor home is not such a charming prospect," Darcy said, drily. Richard rather felt as if he spoke from experience, and recalled how distant and quiet Pemberley must be when Darcy was there alone, or with just his sister for company. The man had never been gregarious, and visitors were a matter of politeness rather than interest for him.

"Who says I wish to set up home as a bachelor?"

This brought his cousin up short, and Darcy fixed him with a curious glance.

"I did not realise you had formed an attachment to any -"

"Oh I haven't," Richard said, cursing his mouth for running on unchecked. How could he admit to his level-headed cousin that he had thought only abstractly of marriage until very recently - that is, until precisely the moment he had laid eyes on Mary Bennet. It was true, she was not beautiful in the conventional sense of the word, but then Richard was aware enough of his own flaws to know that he would never be considered handsome. He did not possess wealth enough to transform his looks, either, for whilst women might be willing to overlook a heavy brow or crooked nose if the man who possessed them were worth ten thousand pounds a year, they were lamentably less willing to do so for a mere Colonel of the regiment, even one who had made a comfortable income from his efforts. He had had his heart broken once already, and was not eager to re-tread that path. But in Mary Bennet, he had noticed something he had been missing in his time surrounded by the harsh world of the militia. She had a quietness and a sweetness about her that would make home something he could begin to imagine. The invisible wife he had once dreamed of keeping a home for him now also contributed to the sounds of melodies that floated through the halls of his imagined home, and fixed him with intelligent grey eyes, eager to hear what he had to say and not inclined to miss when he made an error. He had noticed this same keen sense of intelligence in both Bennet sisters he had met at Netherfield, albeit rather more clearly developed in Elizabeth than Jane, who he thought too sweet-natured to be real, somehow, which rendered her perfect for simple, good-tempered Charles Bingley.

"I am sure our aunt will only be too happy to take the matter into consideration," Darcy remarked, with a faint smile. "Should you wish her to."

Richard refused to dignify that with a response, merely urged his horse into motion once more.

"We have stayed still too long, Darcy. Come, let's ride over to that ridge over yonder."

He did not wait for his cousin's reply, but set off at a pace, wishing to blow away some of the thoughts that now started to crowd in on him. How was it possible that he was thinking of marriage, that he was thinking at all of a young woman he had laid eyes on but once? He did not know her at all, and certainly, she could not think in any particular way about him. He was setting himself up for a fall and would die before he admitted his folly to his cousin, or to anybody else.

Chapter Six

"Jane, you look beautiful as always!" Elizabeth sang, taking a moment to admire her elder sister before turning her attention to her own reflection.

Mary hung back near the door, shyly wondering what right she had to be in the room with her two elder sisters and wishing she had refused Jane's invitation with more determination.

"There! Now, Mary, it is your turn!"

Mary wondered if her intent to leave had been audible, for it to attract Jane's attention so decidedly. She frowned, and glanced, worriedly, at Elizabeth, but was surprised to see her smile matched Jane's.

"I have had a lot of practice in wrangling unruly curls into elegant style," Lizzy said, brandishing a handful of hairpins. "And so, Mary, I turn my attention to you!"

This thinly veiled threat of torture was accompanied with a laugh, and the gentle escort of her sister, who tugged Mary into a seat in front of the mirror, so she might watch their progress.

"I don't see any need for all this fuss -" Mary began.

"Fuss? What fuss?" Jane dismissed her. "Now, sit still, while I check your gown. If it belonged to Elizabeth there is every chance there will be a tear in it somewhere, or a stain, or some - ow!"

Elizabeth had turned her attention away from Mary for half a second to give her sister a punishing pinch in return for her comments about the state of her clothing, never mind the fact that it was generally true that Elizabeth's gowns suffered from her romping ways.

"It looks very pretty on you, Mary. I am glad you will be wearing it this evening," Elizabeth said, jamming a pin into Mary's scalp, and muttering a hasty apology before Mary had time to wonder if it was intentional.

"Surely Lydia and Kitty will need help as well…" Mary ventured.

"Lydia and Kitty?" Elizabeth snorted. "The only help they will need is in wearing marginally less finery to what is only a dinner, but Mama will see to that. You know they spend half their lives preening before a mirror anyway, so one more evening will offer little in the way of challenge to them.

Mary smiled, pleased not to be on the receiving end of Elizabeth's scornful assessment for once. Or rather, not merely for once. It seemed to her that Elizabeth had grown altogether pleasanter to her in the past few days. Last afternoon, when Mary had made a recommendation to her sisters, Elisabeth had even hushed Lydia's outcry, in order that they might all listen to what Mary had to say. She had thanked her for sharing her opinion, and agreed that they would all do well to follow Mary's example and dwell a little more on charity and a little less on hair-ribbons.

Jane, too, had actually sought her out for company, bringing with her a piece of sheet music that was giving her particular trouble and asking whether Mary, being the more skilled of the two, would very much object to sitting with her for ten minutes and helping her to learn it. Their ten minutes had become a happy hour, where Mary showed off her skills on the piano, at Jane's prompting, and blushed happily under her sister's hearty applause.

"I hope you intend to play for us this evening, Mary," Jane said, as if she, too, recalled the meeting, and wished to bring it to mind again.

"I am sure everyone will be eager to hear you," Elizabeth agreed. "For goodness knows they shall not wish to hear me! Jane may venture a piece, and I dare say Caroline Bingley will play something, but you are the real songbird of the house, Mary, and must not be too shy to demonstrate."

This was the closest thing to a true compliment that Mary had ever received from her sister, and she was so shocked at it that she turned around in her seat, causing Elizabeth to move with her, in order to pin one last offending curl in place.

"Why are you being so nice to me"? she asked, glancing across at Jane as well. "I cannot imagine I deserve it, and cannot think what has happened to change your opinion of me so drastically in so short a time."

"Change our opinion?" Jane laughed and patted Mary warmly on the arm. "When have we ever not had a fond opinion of you, dear?"

Every day of my life, Mary thought. She was afraid to voice it, in case the admission ended this current period of felicity.

"Jane!" Mrs Bennet's voice called upstairs, and ever-obedient, Jane hurried down to see what was the matter. Mary stood to follow after her but Elizabeth laid a hand on her arm, staying her progress for half a moment.

"Mary," she murmured. "I am sorry if you have ever thought I did not care for you as a sister, or as a friend."

Mary blinked at her, quite shocked to hear such words coming from her sister's lips.

"I know we are not very alike, but I do not see why that means we must be at odds. I hope - I hope we can try a little harder to find some common ground in the future."

This little speech may have been short, but it was uttered with feeling and conveyed much, much more than its direct content. Impulsively, Mary threw her arms around her sister, not trusting herself to speak. She, too, had not always been particularly gracious towards Elizabeth. She had dismissed her as silly on many occasions, albeit not as silly as Kitty and Lydia. She had been jealous of her confidence, for little ever seemed to shake Elizabeth out of being just exactly who she was. Mary, on the other hand, constantly felt as if she were singing from a hymn sheet in a slightly different key to everybody else, and it took all her will to keep to their tune.

"I do not always make it easy to love me, I know," she muttered, while they embraced so that she could talk to the back of Elizabeth's head and not be forced to look at her while she spoke. "But I am very glad that you are my sister."

"Girls!" Mrs Bennett's voice squawked. "Come along or we shall very likely be late! Kitty, Lydia, you must surely be ready by now! Elizabeth! Mary, do come along!"

With a shared laugh at their mother's anxiety, the two girls hurried down, and Mary felt a flicker of excitement about the evening that lay ahead and a growing affection for the sisters who would accompany her.

THE SITTING ROOM AT Netherfield was busy, and Darcy was grateful to find a quiet corner he could keep to himself. Colonel Fitzwilliam was eager to meet everyone Bingley introduced him to, being almost as gregarious and outgoing as his friend, and even Caroline Bingley was fortunately occupied with her guests, so Darcy was afforded some peace and the ability to observe events without being forced to be a part of them too much at present.

The doors flew open to admit the Bennet family, headed by an enthusiastic Mrs Bennet and her rather more reluctant husband, whose eyes met Darcy's in a moment of shared understanding. With the addition of eight extra people, the volume of conversations in the small room increased dramatically. Darcy could barely refrain from rolling his eyes at the way Charles burst forward, claiming Jane Bennet's attention almost immediately, and forsaking all his other guests, as if she were the only other person in the room. What stopped Darcy in his tracks was to see almost the same behaviour, albeit on a far less enthusiastic scale, pass over his cousin, who greeted each of the Bennets politely in turn as they were introduced to him, but returned almost immediately to one in particular. *Mary*, Darcy recalled her name although he was not sure he had spoken to her even once before. She was the musical one, the middle daughter, less engaging than Jane or, Darcy was forced to grudgingly admit, Elizabeth, but equally not as grating as the younger two, who were at present running rings around Caroline whose smile became increasingly like a grimace as their questions continued. Had

Darcy's attention not been so caught up with Richard, he might have found Caroline's predicament amusing. As it was, he had been so intrigued by his cousin's apparent interest in the middle Miss Bennet that he did not notice her sister moving towards his corner and thus startled when he noticed her.

"Miss Elizabeth." He bowed, recalling to mind his manners almost immediately and covering his surprise with a faint smile.

"Mr Darcy." Elizabeth smiled back and Darcy was surprised to note how charming she looked that evening, how the deep green of her dress complimented her dark hair and made her features warm in the flickering candlelight. She glanced over her shoulder as if to assure herself that Darcy had observed what she had, before speaking of it. "It seems your cousin and my sister are already well acquainted!"

"Indeed," Darcy replied.

"I think them a fine pair, for see how my sister Mary blossoms under his attention."

This Darcy had not seen, for his eyes had been entirely for his cousin. Looking again he had to acknowledge that Elizabeth was right. Mary, who had always seemed pale and dull to him, on the rare occasion he had had cause to notice her at all, positively glowed as Colonel Fitzwilliam quizzed her on some matter of interest to them both. This stumped Darcy entirely. What could his cousin, Colonel of the regiment, possibly find to talk to Miss Mary Bennet about that made them both smile so freely? He shifted his position, awkwardly, envying his cousin his easy manner among strangers. Whilst Darcy might be the wealthier, the more handsome, the better educated and more elegant of the two, Richard Fitzwilliam had always been the more popular in company. He was better able to manage both his temper and his manners, and found it altogether easier to address strangers than Darcy ever had. It was the one thing he envied his cousin for. He thought back over their earlier conversations, recalling that not being considered worthy marriage material for Anne, Richard was free of a large measure of Lady Catherine's interferences, and his frown darkened. Two things he envied his cousin. But two things, only.

"You do not seem pleased." It was a statement, not a question, but Darcy felt compelled to answer her anyway.

"I am neither pleased nor displeased. My cousin is a free man, and he may speak to whomever he wishes."

"Even if that is the middle daughter of a less-than-prestigious country family." Elizabeth bristled under this implied slight, and Darcy hurried to counter it once more, not wishing to begin the evening with an argument, although unsure if he and Elizabeth Bennet would ever manage half an hour together without descending into disagreement.

"I did not say such a thing, Miss Elizabeth, I merely meant -"

"I know what you meant, Mr Darcy. You wear your opinions quite frankly on your features, so you need not worry yourself with explaining them." Elizabeth smiled as she spoke, to suggest a joke, but there was a flash of anger in her dark eyes.

"Whereas, Miss Elizabeth, you hide your own behind a smile and good humour, so one can never feel himself entirely certain of your meaning."

Elizabeth was taken aback, and Darcy felt a flicker of pride at the way her smile faltered for just a moment. He was about to speak again, when Caroline Bingley joined them.

"Well, this is a comfortable corner you have found for yourself, Mr Darcy. Miss Elizabeth, your two youngest sisters are as charming as ever!" She laid an emphasis on the word *charming* which plainly indicated she thought the exact opposite of Kitty and Lydia, and Darcy detected a flare of irritation in Elizabeth's features that made him actually feel a moment of kindness towards her. She would not choose to speak against her own sisters, feeling that inescapable loyalty one feels towards one's own family, yet he rather felt that she did not think altogether highly of the giddy and excitable Kitty and Lydia, and so her reaction was tempered with a broad smile.

"They certainly seem fond of you, Miss Bingley. How fortunate that you have managed to win two friends for yourself amongst Hertfordshire society."

Darcy had to choke back his own amused reaction to this response, which had suggested entirely by implication that Caroline had made nought but these two young friends during her time thus far in Hertfordshire. Caroline did not respond straight away, and Darcy gathered that she was weighing her options, struggling to decide whether to take Elizabeth to task for her insult, and thus be forced to acknowledge it, or to ignore it. At length, she decided on the latter, and merely smiled.

"Your other younger sister, Mary, isn't it? She certainly seems enchanting this evening. I believe I recognise the dress she is wearing as one I have seen gracing your frame before now."

There was another thinly veiled insult, and Darcy felt a little affronted on the Bennets' behalf. It was plain to all that the family were not extravagantly wealthy, yet to remark upon their mode of dress was of the utmost bad taste. Darcy saw Elizabeth freeze, and decided to intervene.

"It suits her most admirably," he said. "And I think it speaks to her excellent character that she seeks to make my cousin feel welcomed here. He has been so rarely in society of late that it is a blessing to see him so at ease, and I am indebted to your family for making him feel so."

This was perhaps the longest speech Darcy had uttered in Elizabeth's presence for some time, and he was pleased to see its effects lightening her features into a faint, surprised smile.

"Miss Elizabeth, I fear you were only fleetingly introduced to my cousin the other day and I do wish for people to know him. Please permit me to make another introduction."

Ignoring Caroline entirely, Darcy offered Elizabeth his arm, and was gratified when she took it, feeling a momentary thrill at the comfortable way they fitted together. He risked another glance at Elizabeth, but saw that her gaze was already fixed on Richard and Mary, and he looked away again quickly.

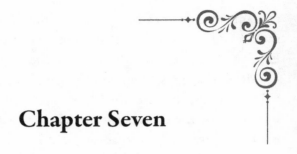

Chapter Seven

"I do hope you will play for us this evening, Miss Mary," Richard said, grateful that he had managed to hold his own in a conversation dominated by music, despite knowing very little about it himself. He had snatched a glance at the sheet music that laid atop the Netherfield piano and tried to cement a few of the terms in his mind. *Andante Cantabile*. He had no idea what it meant but the very word sounded like music when he repeated it in his mind. He certainly did not trust himself to use it yet, for he doubted his pronunciation and was certain he would only make a fool of himself if he tried to sound intelligent, but perhaps Mary would use it herself and then he might learn from her.

"I would like to," she said, shyly. "If I am asked, and if there is the opportunity."

Jane Bennet, who had been standing nearby with Charles Bingley, seized upon this and joined their conversation.

"I am sure everyone would love to hear you, Mary." She lifted her gaze to Colonel Fitzwilliam with a warm smile. "My sister is definitely the most musical of all of us, so if anyone is to provide music it must be her!"

"Then you must play, Miss Mary, and the rest of us can dance!" Charles cried, rejoicing at this potential plan. Richard was a fraction less animated at the prospect.

"Do you not like to dance, Miss Mary?"

Mary shook her head, a dark flush staining her cheeks.

"I am not very good at it," she confessed. "And in any case, I prefer to play the music than dance to it."

Richard nodded, swallowing his disappointment. He had half-hoped he might be permitted to ask his new friend to dance and then be able to get to know her a little better. Although he was surprised at the speed and depth of his feelings, he was left to guess at Mary Bennet's. Surely she could not view him in the same way, for they had scarcely even spoken to one another. Yet he felt as if they had known each other far longer, for already her features were familiar to him and he felt that he understood her better than some people he had known his whole life.

"I am sure, Mary, you would do Colonel Fitzwilliam the honour of dancing, if he were to ask you," Jane prompted, sharing a glance with her sister that Richard did not understand, nor did he try to. There was a moment's awkward silence, and Charles weighed in with his own opinion, fervently wedded to Jane's.

"Indeed! For I am sure Mr Darcy has already claimed Miss Elizabeth's hand for a dance, so you must do his cousin the honour too. Caroline will happily play for us at least once, will not you, sister?"

Richard glanced up quickly enough to see Caroline's face fall into a scowl, although she recovered her peace fairly quickly, and agreed that she would play a piece or two, if everybody else was bound and determined to dance. Her voice took on a mournful tone as she said this, and Richard noticed the look she darted towards Darcy, who was standing to one side conversing with Elizabeth Bennet and entirely oblivious to their discussion. This, too, brought Richard to a pause, for he was quite sure he had never yet seen his cousin so content, and in speaking to a young lady! He blinked, sure the apparition was a fabrication and one that would vanish given proper attention. Instead, it solidified into fact, before his very eyes, and a sly smile of recognition crept onto his face. Darcy might have claimed indifference in their conversation, but the glimmer of light he had recognised in his cousin's eyes was anything but indifferent. Tilting his head slightly, he regarded Elizabeth more carefully. She was pretty, although no sister could compete with Jane in terms of beauty. In fact, he recognised far more in common between Elizabeth and Mary than either sister had with Jane, possessing the same dark colouring and determined chin. Elizabeth's features were somewhat sharper, her eyes darting this way and that, her perpetual smile giving her face an animation lacking in Mary's more sanguine features. *She will certainly keep Darcy on his toes,* Richard thought, acknowledging how well it would suit his cousin to have a clever wife, whose character might force him into improvement, rather than one like dear Anne, who would never think of challenging him. Richard loved both of his cousins equally, but he knew them well enough to acknowledge their utter incompatibility. Their only common characteristic was a desire for quiet and solitude, yet whilst that suited Anne's delicate nature and ailing health, it did little for Darcy but to make him morose. When he had heard his cousin would be staying in Hertfordshire with friends, he rejoiced at the notion of Darcy being among friends, but tempered that with an anxiety that could not be shaken: surely London was a better place for his cousin, where it would be difficult for him to find the isolation that would come far too easily in the country. It was his second excuse for this visit, though he'd never dream of admitting as much to Darcy, that he was concerned for his well-being and determined to check up on him for himself. He had not considered, even after their reunion, that the ideal woman for his cousin might reside here, in Hertfordshire, and that this short visit to the countryside might be the very best thing for either cousin.

"Colonel Fitzwilliam?"

Jane's direct address startled Richard out of his reverie, and he forced his attention back to the present.

"Forgive me, Miss Bennet, I did not hear your question," he said, upon noticing the circle viewing him with expectation, waiting for his response.

"I was asking if you would tell us a little of your travels with the regiment. Mr Bingley tells me you have been abroad?"

Richard nodded, risking a glance at Mary. He had various stories chosen, ready for just such an occasion as this, and was well-practiced in tailoring his tales to his audience. Whilst Bingley would no doubt rejoice in heroics and daring, he found himself speaking rather more gently, of the beauty of the mountains, the hospitality of local people and the interesting tastes in food he had experienced while he was away. Jane Bennet was delighted, and peppered his account with questions. Fearing he had already bored Mary, which was the exact opposite of his intent, he risked a glance at her, and was surprised and touched to see the careful attention she paid him, the way her eyes were fixed in his direction. Their eyes met for half a moment, before she dropped her gaze, but Richard was warmed to see the half-smile that played about her lips, and began to hope that maybe, just maybe, he was not so vain in his hopes after all. *She cannot possibly care for me yet, but perhaps she might learn to...*

ELIZABETH WAS SURPRISED by the way Darcy had rallied to her defence and not only hers but her sister's, when she doubted he had ever spoken or even acknowledged Mary before now other than to group her with the rest of the Bennets as beneath his notice. She was surprised, too, by the enthusiasm he had professed in wishing to introduce her to Colonel Fitzwilliam properly, and his insistence in accompanying her. There was something more than practised politeness behind this, and the way in which he escorted her to the growing party that surrounded his cousin. Elizabeth was pleased to spot not only Mary but also Jane and Mr Bingley, all engaged in conversation with Colonel Fitzwilliam, who appeared to be telling an interesting story from his time with the regiment.

"Were you not afraid?" Jane's voice carried, as they drew nearer.

"Afraid? My cousin?" Darcy scoffed. "I rather venture he thrives on fear, for he's hardly had a day's peace and quiet this past year."

"That must be difficult," Mary ventured, and Elizabeth was touched to see the concern etched on her younger sister's features.

"It is no better or worse than the fate afforded any soldier," Colonel Fitzwilliam said, with a philosophical shrug. "And I am grateful, now, to take a little time to rest before I press on to Kent."

"Kent!" There was a squawk from elsewhere in the room, and before anybody could speak again, Mr Collins had thrust himself into the centre of the group. "You speak of Kent, Colonel Fitzwilliam?" He laughed. "But of course you do! I do not doubt you are eager to see your aunt again. Are you aware that she is my patroness, and oh, what a fine, elegant, generous..."

"Richard, I wished to introduce Miss Elizabeth Bennet to you." Mr Darcy spoke as if he was not even aware of Mr Collins, and his voice was so commanding that it forced the simpering curate into deferent silence.

At this close proximity, Elizabeth was forced to acknowledge her sister's accuracy. Colonel Fitzwilliam and Mr Darcy were not entirely unlike each other, although another thought overtook her quite before she was aware she had thought it: Darcy was markedly the more handsome. Very slightly taller, very slightly slimmer, there was something about the combination of features and dark colouring that worked to form a rather more elegant picture in Darcy than it did in Colonel Fitzwilliam. However, when the latter turned to greet Elizabeth with a warm, genuine smile, her surprising affection for Mr Darcy vanished. Oh, if only he would smile as easily as his cousin did! Still, now, he seemed mildly displeased by some state of affairs she could not determine, and his lips settled into a perpetual line.

"I am so pleased to meet you again, Miss Elizabeth," Colonel Fitzwilliam said. "I see you have quite captured my cousin. I do hope you were not discussing your evening's companions?"

Beside her, Darcy straightened, and Elizabeth felt him hurrying to summon a response, but stilling any comment from him, she laughed, taking Colonel Fitzwilliam's observation for what it was: a joke.

"Ah yes, we were deep in discussion over how a Colonel in the regiment could have managed to get himself lost on his arrival in Hertfordshire. If this is a comment on the skills of our military, ought we to fear for our future as a nation?"

Colonel Fitzwilliam roared with laughter, delighted with this comment, and Lizzy was amazed at how different he was from his cousin. Even though she had spoken in a teasing tone and made plain that she did not mean her comment at all seriously, had she made such an observation to Mr Darcy it would surely have been taken with irritation, as a personal criticism. His cousin slapped his knee, and remarked that a man was only as good as the directions he was given.

"I assure you my directions were accurate, had you actually read them," Darcy muttered. When Elizabeth looked at him, disappointed to see her assessment of him proved accurate, she was instead surprised to note a smile tugging at his usually glum features.

"First my navigation and now my literacy is under attack!" Colonel Fitzwilliam held his hands up in mock surrender. "And yet my cousin invites me here *amongst friends!*" He shook his head in amused disbelief. "I question your definition of the word."

"I am surprised to hear Mr Darcy refer to any of us as friends," Elizabeth said, unable to resist the chance to nettle Mr Darcy further, now he appeared to be in a humour to take it. "For he has been anything but welcoming to certain of us. But perhaps you did not mean to include myself or my sisters in your assessment, and saved your compliments for Mr and Miss Bingley alone."

"I did not mention you at all," Darcy admitted, then realised that this might be taken as a slight, and hastened to explain further. "That is, I referred only to those in residence at Netherfield, as they alone would have their daily lives interrupted by my cousin's arrival."

"You did not bargain on my stumbling unintentionally into Longbourn and interrupting your neighbours of my own accord," Colonel Fitzwilliam countered, with a smile. "And yet, see what a fine party my error has brought together."

"A fine party that really ought to see about moving into the dining room." Caroline's arch voice carried easily over the comfortable chatter, and Elizabeth detected a clear note of annoyance at how fondly her guests seemed to be conversing. "Mr Darcy, perhaps you would be so kind as to escort me into dinner, for I see my brother is already poised to accompany Miss Bennet."

With all politeness, but an evident reluctance, Mr Darcy fell obediently into place beside Caroline, and Elizabeth found herself free to walk in with Colonel Fitzwilliam, which state of affairs did not entirely displease her.

"You appear to successfully run rings around my cousin, Miss Elizabeth," he said, in a low, teasing tone. "A fact for which I must applaud you. He is not usually so easily managed."

"Easily?" Elizabeth shook her head. "If you think I am capable of managing such a gentleman, I must disabuse you of that notion immediately. Alas, our acquaintance did not get off to the best of starts."

"Yet you seem quite agreeable to one another now," Colonel Fitzwilliam pressed. "I am pleased, for Darcy needs people who know their own mind. Darcy is too used to having his own way, with nobody to challenge him."

Elizabeth awes silent for a moment, digesting this detail before responding to it.

"You care deeply for your cousin, Colonel." She smiled. "It is admirable to see."

"Admirable, nothing! He is the best of men, but he is not without flaws. Are not all of us?"

"Indeed," Elizabeth mused, catching sight of Mary, as she was seated nearby, and rethinking the many unkind things she had said to her sister over the years. Her conscience convicted her, and she frowned, which did not go unnoticed by Colonel Fitzwilliam.

"I fear I have said something to upset you, Miss Elizabeth. You must allow for an old soldier, too ill-acquainted of late with society, to make the occasional conversational misstep."

"Can the truth ever be considered a misstep?"

Elizabeth's voice softened as she spoke, for she recalled another man's words, muttered in confidence to his friends and never intended to be overheard by the woman they concerned. She had held Darcy's words against him since first meeting the man, and still now her pride smarted at the way he had dismissed her. Yet had his words been untrue? Or did she just rail against them, *because* of their truth?

"Perhaps not," Colonel Fitzwilliam conceded. "Yet I hardly think sermonizing an apt occupation for a dinner."

He cast a wry glance across the table to where Mr Collins sat, ably doing just that and serving the weary looking Mr Bennet with his own personal treatise on the morality of wine at dinner.

Smiling at Colonel Fitzwilliam, Elizabeth turned away, but not before noticing the way her new friend's eyes strayed over to where Mary sat, quietly observing all that unfolded around her.

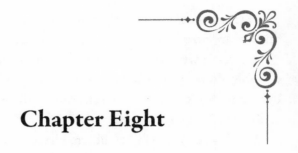

Chapter Eight

Mary's eyes travelled around the table, grateful that the candlelight, and being seated where she was afforded the chance to observe everyone's interactions without being unduly pressured to join in with any conversations herself.

Once more, in spite of her best efforts to avoid him, she found her gaze straying to Colonel Fitzwilliam, who just presently was engaged in conversation with his cousin, Mr Darcy, and Elizabeth, who was laughing as he told them a particularly amusing story of life in the regiment. Mary felt a flash of envy that it was to her sister he addressed his tale, and not her, and then a further flash that Elizabeth was able to so easily comport herself in public. Did she not worry that her laugh, unchecked, would draw attention? Did she not care that when she held up a hand to pause Colonel Fitzwilliam in his telling, to bid him explain some point to her in finer detail, that he might think her stupid and cease speaking altogether? Mary's eyes narrowed, and she watched her sister carefully, wondering how Elizabeth managed to be so entirely herself, utterly without artifice. She, Mary, was so often on edge that she preferred to hide away behind the piano, or in the shadows, lest she be noticed at all, for surely it would not be a good noticing. Her attention on the group was such that her attempts to remain invisible slipped, just for a moment, but it was precisely at that moment that Colonel Fitzwilliam paused for breath, lifting his eyes and meeting hers.

"I fear I am scandalising your sister," he said, his lips lifting in a grin. "Pray, Miss Mary, do not judge me too harshly, and recall that in military service a gentleman's manners are apt to slip once in a while."

Mary smiled, feeling instinctively that he was making a joke, although she had missed its context entirely, and her smile faltered as soon as it began, as she wondered after all whether it was the right response. It must have been, for her smile caused Colonel Fitzwilliam's to widen, and she felt a flicker of delight as he moved to include her in their conversation.

"Mary has a great interest in foreign countries," Elizabeth asserted. "She is far more educated than I."

"Have you travelled, Miss Mary?"

Despite the use of her name, it took Mary a moment to realise the question was addressed to her, and she glanced helplessly at Elizabeth, who hurried to her aid.

"Unfortunately we none of us have travelled widely, except in books." She smiled apologetically. "Although we have family in London and have been there often, have we not, Mary? My sister adores music, as you know, Colonel Fitzwilliam, and so we take every advantage of hearing it when we are in town."

"Ah, you would have a great deal in common with my cousin, Georgiana," Colonel Fitzwilliam said, with a slight nod towards Mr Darcy. "Is that not right, Darcy? Georgiana is very musical."

"What a pity she is not here as well, Mary, and then you might meet! For unfortunately she bores her sisters - that is, we none of us are talented enough to understand her when she speaks." Elizabeth smiled, covering her almost-criticism ably.

"It is another language to me, entirely!" Colonel Fitzwilliam said, clearing his throat. "Andante. Now, really! It is a very pretty word, but I am at a loss to understand it."

"It's really very easy," Mary began. "It means "moderately slow" in Italian."

"And it sounds far more musical than our one-syllable "slow"," Colonel Fitzwilliam remarked. "I had no idea you spoke Italian as well, Miss Mary. Truly you Bennet sisters are a force to be reckoned with."

"Oh, I don't -"

"Mary is certainly the most educated of us all," Elizabeth continued. "For she regularly studies Fordyce's sermons as well." She smiled at Colonel Fitzwilliam. "Are you familiar with them?"

"I confess my ignorance," he said, with a comical shrug. "But that is -"

"My dear Colonel!" A silly laugh punctuated the colonel's comment, and Mr Collins leaned over the table towards them. Do I hear you make reference to the sermons of Fordyce?"

Elizabeth groaned, almost indiscernibly, and turned with an affectation of brightness towards their cousin.

"We do, Mr Collins, but unfortunately we will not dwell on them, for Colonel Fitzwilliam is not overly familiar with them, and in any case, they are hardly fit conversation for the dinner table." This last was muttered under her breath, and caused a sly smile to pass between Mr Darcy and his own cousin.

"Not fit conversation!" Mr Collins blustered. "Why, one must always be concerned with one's spiritual formation, Miss Elizabeth. As I was so very recently saying to my patroness, Lady Catherine - oh!" He giggled. "Forgive me, your aunt, who is, you know, a very fastidious woman..."

"That reminds me, Mr Collins," Colonel Fitzwilliam said, taking his opportunity as the worthy curate paused for breath to take hold of the conversation once more and prevent it being utterly derailed by mention of Lady Catherine and her opinion of Fordyce any longer. "My aunt is also a great lover of music, although she does not play..."

Mary had sunk back into her chair, feeling herself dismissed by Colonel Fitzwilliam's dismissal of Fordyce. He plainly thought the book of sermons dull - and no doubt anybody who valued them as she did would likewise be considered thus. So to hear her own name on his lips once more brought her up sharply.

"Miss Mary, perhaps you will advise me of some music I might mention to her. Her daughter plays, and I should like to suggest some new pieces for her to look out for, but am thoroughly behind on what is fashionable at present."

"I do not know that I have any notion of what is fashionable -" Mary began, doubtfully.

"Oh, but you have such taste, Mary!" Elizabeth countered. "Yes, Colonel Fitzwilliam, I do not doubt Mary will be more than happy to help you choose some music to take to Rosings with you. In fact -" she paused, and Mary thought she could detect the wheels turning in Elizabeth's mind as she pieced her plan together. "We had already planned to walk into Meryton tomorrow, Mary and I, and Jane, of course. Perhaps you and Mr Darcy would consider accompanying us?"

DARCY WAS HARDLY IN a position to refuse the invitation to Meryton, nor did he, at that moment, wish to. He was surprised to feel himself actually cheering a little at the suggestion of the trip, which emotion gave him pause. He cared little enough for Meryton itself, having been there once or twice and been underwhelmed by its small collection of streets and shops. This time, though, the suggestion of a visit struck him as a particularly pleasant notion.

"There is a regiment stationed there, I believe?" Colonel Fitzwilliam queried.

"Indeed!" Elizabeth laughed. "I cannot believe I did not think to mention that. Perhaps you will have colleagues there that you wish to reconnect with."

"Perhaps." Richard grimaced, and Darcy did not need further explanation to understand his thoughts. Wickham was rumoured to be amongst them, and Richard had little enough desire to meet the man again. Although his association with Wickham had been far more fleeting than Darcy's own, he was the one man, aside from Darcy himself, who knew something of Wickham's attempts to seduce and elope with Georgiana, and he would neither forget nor forgive such behaviour. "In fact, I would like to see the Colonel...I believe it is a Colonel Foster, for I have some intelligence regarding a member of his regiment that I rather fancy he would do well to be made aware of."

Richard glanced up then, sharing a wordless glance with Darcy that intimated Wickham was on his mind, and he intended to illuminate the man's chequered past to his new Colonel. Darcy certainly did not object to such a plan, even more so if it encouraged Wickham to move on from Meryton. He would not rest easy in the knowledge such a man was stationed so close by, and his presence additionally ensured he would not dream of fetching Georgiana down, no matter how many fond invitations he received on her behalf, or how many pleasant young ladies he might find hereabouts that would make a companion for her.

The tension caused at the mention of the regiment had allowed a natural silence to fall over the small group, which was presently interrupted by Caroline Bingley, who evidently tired of Jane Bennet and her brother, and, caring little for her other guests, turned to Mr Darcy in an attempt to engage him in conversation.

"What topic has you all so quiet?" she asked, with a laugh. "Surely Miss Eliza cannot be boring you with tales of her most recent walk!" Her snide comment would have made most women flinch, but Elizabeth merely lifted her chin, meeting Caroline's gaze with a broad smile.

"Not at all, Miss Bingley. Colonel Fitzwilliam and Mr Darcy were just speaking of his sister, who sounds an utterly charming young lady." Darcy bit his tongue, discerning, if Caroline did not, that whilst Elizabeth might think Georgiana "utterly charming", she certainly did not find her hostess so.

"Ah, yes! Dear, dear Georgiana! She must be quite tall now, Mr Darcy. As tall as you, I do not doubt!" She laughed at a joke that was neither clever nor funny.

"No," Darcy said, drily. "Yet I would say that she approaches Miss Elizabeth's height, although that is where their physical similarities end."

"Oh, yes, for Georgiana has the most beautiful golden hair and such a fair complexion..." Caroline continued. "Not at all like you, Eliza, dear."

"We cannot all be blessed with beauty, although we might all of us work to improve our character."

This quiet comment Darcy thought, at first, came from Elizabeth. It was to his great surprise to realise that it had been Mary, not her sister, who thus ended Caroline's veiled barbs, for after a moment of confusion, feeling certain she had been slighted although unable to distinguish how, Caroline sniffed, and turned away, aiming to engage one of the young gentlemen who had thus far been captivated with the young Miss Bennets in conversation.

"Do you see what I mean, Colonel Fitzwilliam?" Elizabeth remarked, with a smile. "My sister is wise beyond her years, and far more able to stand her own ground than even I give her credit for."

A glance passed between the two ladies, and Darcy felt a flash of approval for their warm relationship. Beneath the differences any sisters might possess there was a deep affection there, and it warmed his heart to see it. Again, for the second time in as many days, he regretted the snap judgment he had made of Elizabeth Bennet, and repented of ever thinking ill of her. Widely different was the Elizabeth Bennet he saw before him now, and his opinion of her was improved by her relations, rather than denigrated by it. His lips quirked. He would never rejoice in such a family as she possessed, but seeing her manage them, and the character such managing indicated, raised her higher in his estimations. He thought of his own relatives, and let out a breath he had not been aware of holding.

"Are we keeping you from something, Mr Darcy?" Elizabeth asked, her eyes sparkling with fun.

Darcy straightened, shaking his head, and feeling his familiar frown settle back over his features. Was she so attuned to him that every mood must be remarked upon? He felt his irritation rise, but then noticed it was good humour and not criticism that had sparked such a comment, and hurried to summon up some sort of response, for surely her question demanded it.

"I rather fancy my cousin is tired of conversing, and anxiously awaits the dancing," Richard remarked, with a sly nudge of Darcy's elbow. "He does so delight in dancing!"

This provoked a still deeper frown, which did not go unnoticed by either lady, and Darcy was at first annoyed at being the butt of the joke. When he saw Elizabeth's eyes stray back to his, though, he thought he detected some interest that he had not noticed there before, and determined to be worthy of it.

"I hope," he said, in a voice low enough that only she might hear it. "That you would do me the honour of dancing with me, Miss Elizabeth. I believe we are long overdue an opportunity."

She paused, and for one deathly moment, Darcy felt certain he had misread her feelings, and braced himself for the scathing refusal that was sure to come. His surprise was palpable, then, when she smiled.

"Certainly, I will dance with you, Mr Darcy. I only hope you can tolerate such a partner."

"And I, you."

He risked a smile and was inordinately gratified to see her return it. *Well, Richard,* he thought, with a cursory glance towards his cousin, who was now heartily demolishing his meal. *I could not have imagined the change your arrival would bring, yet I cannot confess to entirely dislike it.*

Chapter Nine

When the meal was over and everyone returned to the sitting room, Mary was hurried towards the piano by both Jane and Elizabeth, who insisted on her playing "something jolly, that everyone might have the opportunity to appreciate your talent!" This had given Mary pause, for she tended towards slower, more technically complex pieces, to illustrate the hours of practice her mastery of them had taken. It was a pride in her accomplishments, she knew, and a desire for recognition that she ought to have abandoned long ago. Tonight, though, she wished to please the sisters who had been so kind to her and cared little for her skills to be remarked upon, only that everyone might enjoy their evening. She began playing a scotch jig, her fingers running over the keys quickly and ably, and soon the whole party was engaged in dancing, or sitting by and watching the dancers with affection. The piece ended all too quickly, and Mary was pressed to play another.

"Perhaps Miss Mary would like a change from always being seated behind the piano," Caroline Bingley observed, when Mary paused to select a third piece. "After all, there are other ladies who play admirably well. Miss Elizabeth?"

"Actually, Miss Bingley, I have just agreed to dance this next with Mr Darcy," Elizabeth said, sweetly. "But I do think it is only fair that Mary be given an opportunity to dance. Perhaps you will be so kind as to play for us, for I have often heard you remark upon your own fondness for playing."

This, Mary felt certain, had not been Caroline's original plan, but she accepted it with obedience, if not grace. Mary took a step towards the seat occupied by her father, hoping that she might escape the trial of dancing, but before she could manage three steps, Colonel Fitzwilliam appeared beside her.

"I wondered if I might persuade you to dance with me, Miss Mary? As you see I have already been blessed to dance with both of your elder sisters, and if I wish to make the set this evening it is only fair!" His eyes twinkled as he spoke, and Mary deduced from his smooth tone of voice that he was joking. Still, it thrilled her to be asked, and to think of dancing with such a handsome gentleman.

"I - I would like that," she said, her voice faltering a little from anxiety. They took their places beside Elizabeth and Mr Darcy, and Mary was certain that everybody must be able to hear her heart thundering in her chest. How Kitty and Lydia lived for moments such as this, she would never understand. Already the myriad of steps she was to dance crowded in on her, and she feared stumbling. She was so nervous that she missed her first step, but soon made up the mistake, for Caroline played a simple piece that Mary herself had practised often. It had a steady pace, and Mary, familiar with the melody, soon found it easy to know instinctively when to move, if one followed the music. She found it so easy that she began, at length, to relax, and her features settled into a smile.

"I am glad to see you dance almost as well as you play, Miss Mary," Colonel Fitzwilliam said, as they crossed paths.

"Although I venture you are rather fonder of the latter. Am I correct in my deduction?"

"Yes," Mary admitted, with a rueful smile. "I do not dance often, and so I rather fear I am not very good."

"On the contrary, you are a natural!"

The pair parted for a moment before the dance afforded them the opportunity to speak once more.

"I am very grateful for your offer to help me select some music for my cousin and aunt, Miss Mary. It is very generous of you to give up your time."

Mary smiled, but inwardly she wondered what the Colonel could possibly imagine her having to usually take up her time so that surrendering it to him and this errand could be seen as a sacrifice.

"I am always glad to offer my assistance where it might be needed," she said, more to be seen to reply than from any real awareness of her words.

"Yes, I must say I find you a very amiable creature - that is, your whole family, all of your sisters..." Colonel Fitzwilliam trailed off, and hurried ahead with the dance, turning away from Mary a second sooner than was required of him. Mary frowned, thinking she detected some agitation colouring his movements.

I must have said something wrong, she thought, running back over her words once more in her mind, and fearing she had made some error and caused offence to a gentleman she had so wished to please.

Why do you care what Colonel Fitzwilliam thinks of you? a stubborn part of her lectured, silently, but she could summon no answer. She only knew that she did care, very much, what

Hertfordshire's newest arrival might think of her. She had allowed herself to hope, for half a moment only, that it really was she, and not her sisters, that Colonel Fitzwilliam had wanted to see that evening. His attempts to discuss music, when he seemed to understand barely half of what he said, and his insistence that they dance together, Mary had taken for proof of his affection for her, or at least, some shared understanding. Now she realised her folly. He cared for her only as one of many sisters, neighbours and friends to his cousin. If he had singled her out at all, it was only because he was a gentleman, and did not wish to step between Jane and Mr Bingley, or Elizabeth and Mr Darcy. Mary was quiet and shy, but she was not blind to the way Mr Darcy looked at her sister when he was certain of being unobserved. So often overlooked herself, Mary was well able to witness the actions of others without drawing any notice, and she ventured to suppose Mr Darcy possessed some slight affection for Elizabeth, although she could not be sure her sister returned it at present. Colonel Fitzwilliam was evidently loyal to his cousin and sought to give both Jane and Elizabeth as much distance as was polite, leaving Mary his simplest option for conversation and dancing. She sighed. It was hardly a romance for the ages, and she had been silly to imagine he took anything other than a neighbourly interest in her.

"AND HOW DO YOU ENJOY the country dance, Mr Darcy?" Elizabeth ventured, after she and Mr Darcy had danced in silence for what seemed, to Elizabeth, an interminably long time.

"It is pleasant enough," he replied, without commitment.

"And the music," Elizabeth continued. "Miss Bingley chose well in playing such a piece, for it is so much nicer to dance to a piece of music one enjoys."

"Indeed."

With a sigh, Elizabeth gave up and turned her attention to her steps. When Mr Darcy had invited her to dance she had accepted with surprise and curiosity, feeling a smug sort of satisfaction that the man who had once declared her not worthy of his time now sought to dance with her. She had not realised that meant they would spend the duration of the dance in silence, for every attempt she made to spark conversation apparently fell on deaf ears. She cast a sly glance towards Mr Darcy and noticed his perpetual frown descending once more over his features. He was an enigma to her, that much was certain. Just when she dared to think she might understand, that they might pass an evening together and succeed in making polite conversation, he fell once more into silence. She turned her gaze towards Jane, her spirits lifting at the way her sister and Mr Bingley moved and smiled as if neither one could imagine a better partner. Thus cheered, she sought out Mary, and instantly her mood dropped. Mary had never been effusive, but she was likewise not well skilled in hiding her true feelings. She was upset, that much was plain from the way her lip drew together and her eyes remained downcast. Fighting a spark of sisterly compassion, she tried to see if Colonel Fitzwilliam was aware of his young partner's feelings or, and Lizzy fervently hoped this was not the case, if he were the cause of them. He seemed almost as downhearted as Mary, his own cheerful smile nowhere to be seen, and his brow wrinkling in consternation, affording him a more than passing resemblance to his cousin.

"Is something the matter, Miss Elizabeth?" that cousin asked, choosing that particular moment to become perceptive.

"The matter?" Elizabeth forced her features into a smile. "Not at all, Mr Darcy. I only feel..."

"Yes?"

"Is it not more typical for a couple to talk, while they are dancing?"

"Is it?"

He seemed honestly befuddled by this suggestion, and his brow furrowed even deeper into a frown.

"I confess, Miss Elizabeth, I do not dance often, and even less often with people I do not know well."

"You can hardly claim us to be strangers, Mr Darcy!" Elizabeth protested.

"True. What are we then? Acquaintances?"

"We cannot be friends, that much is certain."

Elizabeth said this with a droll tone, in hopes he might take it for humour, for she had felt her own staunch feelings against Mr Darcy softening dramatically in the past few days, in witnessing his close friendship with Charles Bingley and latterly in seeing his interactions with his cousin. She was willing to overlook his comments about her at the Meryton assembly, for certainly, she did not mind him thinking her dull. They could be friends and not remark upon one another's appearance, surely?

"Certain? And why is that?" Mr Darcy asked, but the dance forced them apart for a moment before Elizabeth could reply, a circumstance for which she was happy because it afforded her a moment or two to construct a suitable response.

"I had it on good authority that Mr Darcy cares for but a few people, and cannot imagine him eager to add to that number a group of silly young ladies from the countryside."

This had come out rather more pointed than Elizabeth had intended, and Darcy visibly flinched at her tone and her words. He pursed his lips, as if considering the familiarity of her phrase, and at last recalled its original source as being a conversation they had once shared. He cleared his throat before speaking again.

"You use my own words against me, Miss Elizabeth."

"They are the only ones to which you pay any heed, surely?"

He said nothing, but bowed his head, slightly, acknowledging her point.

They continued to dance in silence, and Elizabeth took the opportunity to seek out Mary once more and was slightly gratified to see the ghost of a smile pass over her younger sister's features. The dance drew to a close, and as Elizabeth turned to curtsey to her partner, she saw only the top of his head, for he bowed, muttered a hasty adieu, and stalked away from her.

Apparently, I have struck a nerve! Elizabeth thought, but she did not feel any sense of rejoicing at such point-scoring. Instead, she felt a wave of guilt. What right had she to brandish a man's past wrongdoings before his face? Surely she would not want her own words, spoken too hastily or in a desire to amuse without due consideration for their implication, thrown back at her?

Determining that she would not let the matter rest, but seek to make good on it, she hurried in the direction Mr Darcy had walked, but had not managed more than two steps before a bulky figure stopped her progress.

"Ah, Miss Elizabeth!" Mr Collins smiled broadly at her. "*Cousin* Elizabeth. I was very much hoping you would do me the honour - the great honour - of dancing this next piece with me. I feel we have not had as much time to converse lately as I might have wished, and dearly hope to rekindle our - ah - early connection."

His eyes twinkled with hidden meaning, and Elizabeth's stomach turned, wishing he would succeed in keeping his meaning rather better hidden. It had been apparent, on Mr Collins' arrival at Longbourn, that he was seeking a wife, and thought a houseful of five daughters a likely place to start. He had even remarked as much over dinner one evening, as if there was nothing disagreeable in declaring himself quite the most eligible bachelor any one of the Bennet sisters could hope to wed. Mrs Bennet had apparently set him straight and declared Jane out of consideration, for, despite her insistence to her husband that Jane and Mr Bingley were merely friends, it was plain to all that this was not a state they would remain in for long, particularly if Mrs Bennet had her way. Mr Collins had quickly and completely shifted his allegiances to Elizabeth, although she had done her best to avoid him, it seemed this was not a sustainable manner in which to live and it would be better to have the dread conversation out of the way.

Not tonight, though! Elizabeth pleaded, darting an anxious glance around at her friends. *Not here!*

"Of course, Mr Collins," Elizabeth said, with a forced smile. "I would be happy to dance with you." Her tone made it clear that this would be all Elizabeth wished to do that evening.

Her misery was completed when she saw Mary slip quietly away to the piano, and would not be pressed to dance again. Caroline Bingley was delighted by this turn of events, although Mr Darcy's propitious disappearance left her to dance with Colonel Fitzwilliam, which state, Elizabeth thought, neither partner relished.

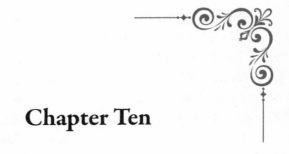

Chapter Ten

Darcy scowled as he retreated through the crowd of dancers and into the corridor, rejoicing only to find himself at last alone, and in quiet, with just the faintest traces of the piano. He was annoyed, but not by Elizabeth Bennet. His annoyance rested solely on his own shoulders. She had thrown his own words back at him, and he could offer no defence. It was an opinion he had formed quickly, as he so often did. Usually, such instincts were rewarded as being accurate. How long, after all, had he held out for Wickham's good, insisting in the face of all the evidence his tenants' reports, that his friend was merely maligned and misunderstood? It had taken Wickham's running away with Georgiana for Darcy to realise his folly, and he had sworn then to always and only trust his first instinct. He had known Wickham's true character as a child and softened to him only at his father's insistence. This was the last gift he could offer the late Mr Darcy, to defend and support his father's godson, and to treat the man as a friend, himself. How had that trust been repaid?

So, yes, Darcy made decisions in an instant. He had grown cautious and was reluctant to trust without some evidence that that trust would be deserved. How much he repented now of his first assessment of Elizabeth Bennet! He might have deemed her unworthy of his attention at Meryton but that was his own prejudice against any woman likely to be showing an interest in him solely on account of his wealth. Was that not the last insult George Wickham had hurled at him? To suggest that Darcy's character, his perpetual bad temper was hardly an enticing prospect for any woman. *How fortunate, William, that you have wealth on your side. Women will flock to you for your pocketbook, and learn to tolerate your mood.* He had thought so of Elizabeth, and in his least generous moments, he still thought so of Jane. It was only when he took the time to notice Charles and Jane Bennet together that he realised there must be some true affection there, and if it was a little stronger on his friend's side than hers, she was sweet tempered enough to grow in affection as their relationship developed. He had ceased to be concerned for Charles' future and determined no longer to stand in the way of their forming any kind of connection. His cousin's comments lodged in his mind. *We all wish to fall in love sometime...there is one easy solution to Aunt Catherine's schemes: marry someone else.* Darcy grimaced. What advice would his expert cousin offer, he wondered, if the woman one could, at last, see oneself marrying was unable to forgive an earlier judgment made in haste, and repented of at leisure?

"Here you are!"

A door behind him swung open, and Charles Bingley appeared in the corridor, concern dimming his usually bright smile. "I feared you were taken ill, with the pace at which you fled the dancing. What on earth has happened?"

"Nothing," Darcy said, with more force than he intended. "Are you not still dancing with Miss Bennet?"

"She wishes to rest, and all the other ladies are occupied at present. My sister and your cousin make a rather uncomfortable pair, but they are not so painful to watch as Miss Elizabeth and Mr Collins!" His eyes widened in amusement. "Poor girl. You must come back and rescue her in time for the next."

"I do not believe Miss Elizabeth will care to dance with me again," Darcy said. *Tonight, or any night.*

"Then you might dance with Caroline and free Colonel Fitzwilliam to do the rescuing." Bingley shrugged, contented with either solution.

Darcy swallowed a groan, not wishing to betray his true feelings for Charles' sister to his face. His reaction must have been evident just the same, for Charles grinned.

"What it is to be so in demand!" He punched Darcy lightly on the arm. "It strikes me the ladies of Hertfordshire must make the most of you while you are here."

"*While I am here?*" Darcy queried. "Do you intend on evicting me?"

"Not I!" Charles was adamant. "You know I would have you stay as long as you wish. But Caroline seems to think you likely to leave when Colonel Fitzwilliam does, and join him in Kent."

Darcy scowled.

"Is everyone intent on planning my time for me and making my decisions as if I am incapable of choosing my own way?"

"Gracious! And who would dream of such a thing?" Charles laughed, clearly a little surprised by the ferocity of Darcy's expression. "If there's one thing I know you, sir, is your ability to know your own mind and follow it absolutely, with no regard for any other's opinion."

"Am I so bull-headed?"

Charles laughed, stopping short when he realised the question was a genuine one.

"Independent," he clarified. "Which is, of itself, no bad thing."

"I am well able to admit when I am wrong," Darcy insisted.

"I do not doubt you capable of anything," Charles agreed. "But I have not often seen it. Fitzwilliam Darcy makes a decision and rarely changes it. His opinions are formed quickly and hold fast. It's why I value your friendship, for I can hardly keep my own mind fixed for more than a day at a time." He glanced around the hallway. "Come, Darcy, let's rejoin the party. You surely cannot intend hiding out here all evening. We'll have them wrap up the dancing in favour of cards and conversation if you prefer it. We must have enough for a few hands of whist, and I'm sure young Miss Mary will happily play something pretty for us to listen to, that is altogether too slow for dancing anyway."

"I do not know that I am in any mood for conversation," Darcy muttered.

"You speak as if that is not usual!" Charles said, darting back to the door before Darcy could register the comment and formulate a response. With a sigh of resignation, he dropped his head and followed his friend back into the hall. Slinking back into the shadows, he was grateful for a moment to observe the dancing without himself being observed. Charles was right: Richard and Caroline did not make a happy pair. She danced with precision, but no grace, and Richard was so busy casting glances towards the piano that he almost missed his steps on more than one occasion, drawing a wrathful glare from his partner. With effort, Darcy lifted his glance to Elizabeth, who was dancing with far more spring in her step than Caroline exhibited, and a patient expression on her face lifted only with the slight air of desperation that flitted across her eyes. Mr Collins appeared to be talking quickly, gripping her hand so tightly that she must be bound to hear him before moving away. Darcy felt a flicker of concern in his chest, and was about to intervene, when Elizabeth wrenched her arm away, hissed something indiscernible to her cousin, and fled the room.

MARY'S PIECE CRASHED to a halt in a chaos of discordant notes.

"Elizabeth?" Mrs Bennet's shrill voice interrupted the sudden silence. "Mr Collins, dear me! What on earth has happened?"

Mr Collins' face was tomato red, and he stammered something almost incoherent. Mary pushed her seat back from the piano, and took a step forward, exchanging a glance with Jane, who also rose, excused herself, and hurried after Elizabeth.

"Well!" Caroline Bingley began, casting a glance around the room with malicious interest. "Poor, dear Eliza! I do hope she has not been taken ill..."

"No, no!" Mrs Bennet said, rushing into the fray with a desperate smile on her face. "I am sure it is nothing to concern you, Miss Bingley. Do, do go back to your dancing. Mary! Play something."

Mary shook her head.

"I don't think -"

"Perhaps you ought to check on her, my dear," Mr Bennet said, with a calming hand on his wife's arm. "I do not imagine any of us are in the mood for more dancing until we have ascertained ourselves of Elizabeth's well-being." He glanced at Mr Bingley. "Perhaps we might have some coffee....?"

"Coffee!" Mr Bingley nodded, enthusiastically. "Yes, yes. Excellent. Coffee! Let us all take some refreshments."

Mary watched as Lydia and Kitty circled closer to Mr Collins, curious to see if they could discover the reason for Elizabeth's sudden flight. Mary wanted to join them, but hung back, not sure whether she ought to check for herself whether Elizabeth was quite well, or whether her presence would even be welcome. Wringing her hands in indecision, she was quite startled to hear a concerned gentlemanly voice near her ear.

"I am sorry to hear your playing interrupted, Miss Mary. I hope your sister is quite well, perhaps merely a little overcome with the heat."

Mary glanced up, smiling gratefully at Colonel Fitzwilliam, who appeared entirely serene in the midst of the chaos. His explanation gave her a lifeline and relief flooded her limbs. The heat! Yes, of course. That must be all that was the matter. Elizabeth had danced longer than she had and with far more energy. No wonder she might be in need of some rest and fresh air.

"I trust you are not similarly overcome?" Colonel Fitzwilliam asked, with concern. "Perhaps we ought to step a little closer to the window."

Gratefully, Mary allowed him to lead her away from the noise of her sisters quizzing Mr Collins. Their cousin's voice had lifted an octave in his insistence that he had said nothing amiss, and Miss Elizabeth was surely merely a little overexcited. This had been sufficient for Lydia and Kitty who were busily discussing how delicate Elizabeth's sensibilities must be if this were true. As they passed Mr Darcy, Mary noticed the scowl he usually wore had receded a fraction, and something that might have been concern rested on his stern features.

"I hope my sister is quite well," she said, glancing towards the door. "Perhaps I ought to go -"

"I believe I saw Miss Bennet and your mother go after her, and am sure they are more than capable of caring for her as she requires. Although, of course, if you wish..."

"No," Mary said, smiling shyly. Her concerns for Elizabeth were still very much present, but she equally did not relish the thought of leaving Colonel Fitzwilliam, particularly when he was being so kind to her.

"Did I ever tell you of my time at the war, Miss Mary?" he asked, after a moment of silence. "The heat there was unbearable, but not like this." He waved his fingers as if to illustrate the dry, smoky heat of the Netherfield parlour. "The sun beat down overhead, and the dirt beneath our feet was white, so it bounced the light back and practically blinded a fellow." He laughed. "Add to that, we would march! Up hill and down, hour after hour, always marching. And dressed in full uniform, with a weapon and pack to carry as well." He shook his head, with a wry smile. "I cannot tell you how much I do *not* miss it!"

Mary's eyes glittered as she tried to imagine the experience Colonel Fitzwilliam described.

"Were you not afraid?" she asked. She had not often thought of the war or what life must be like for members of the militia once they were deployed. Her experience of such men was only when they were stationed at Meryton, and she thought them to be loud, ridiculous young peacocks, always focused purely on having fun and flirting with young ladies, whether they wished to be flirted with or not. Colonel Fitzwilliam was not at all like those young men. There was a calmness to his features, a serious glint in his eyes that suggested some real depth of feeling and she found herself longing to know him better. That he seemed content to speak of it merely encouraged her further.

"Not I!" he said, with a shake of his head. He chuckled. "That is, I was on occasion mildly concerned for my future." He winked "But I'll not admit to that again, Miss Mary, for I do not wish your family to think me a coward!"

"We would never think that!" Mary said, affronted. "Why, I think you brave for choosing such a career in the first place. So many gentlemen wish only stay at home where they might be safe."

"So many men are fortunate enough to have such an occupation open to them!" Colonel Fitzwilliam said, with an unreadable expression on his face. "And many men who enter the regiment do not anticipate seeing action. The majority of our time is spent drilling, and waiting." He shrugged his broad shoulders. "Such a lack of occupation is not always wise for young men, for they are apt to find themselves in mischief without hearty occupation."

"Not if they choose to avoid it," Mary said. "I do not imagine you would ever find yourself in such a circumstance."

"You do me a great honour, Miss Mary, in thinking so well of me. I might remind you we are but a little acquainted and had you ever the misfortune of seeing me often you might change your mind. I can be quite as lazy and bad tempered as any gentleman, although I credit myself with the notion that I do seek to improve."

"That is all that can be asked of any of us."

"I can hardly imagine you have any need of improvement."

This last was murmured so low that Mary was quite sure she had misheard him. When she glanced up at him, she noticed his gaze fixed on her with an intensity that made colour rise in her cheeks.

"Forgive me, I ought not to speak so freely." He cleared his throat. "Look, here is my cousin to join us by the window. Darcy, how do you fare this evening? I was just boring poor Miss Mary with tales of my life overseas. Come and bring some sanity back with your own tales of Pemberley."

Mary felt a flash of annoyance at Mr Darcy, fearing the easy conversation they had been having would be ended with the arrival of Colonel Fitzwilliam's bad tempered cousin. She was surprised, then, to see his features were not quite as fierce as she expected, and when he spoke his tone was gentle.

"I hope you, too, are not upset, Miss Mary? Pray, is your sister quite well?"

"I - I imagine she is," Mary said, her throat dry. She swallowed and continued speaking. "That is, I hope her to be. I did not want to crowd her with too much attention, but perhaps, if neither you nor Colonel Fitzwilliam mind, I will go and check on her myself."

"Please do," Mr Darcy said. "And do ensure that she is aware of our concern."

Chapter Eleven

"Surely you can see how ridiculous the idea is, Mama!"

"The only thing I can see, *Elizabeth,* is how little you care for your own family! Do you wish to see us cast out in the street by that man?"

"Would you rather I marry him?"

Mary had not gone very far down the corridor before the hushed tones of her sisters and mother reached her ears. At the use of the word *marry* her step quickened. This could not be true! Surely everyone was happy to think of Jane marrying Mr Bingley? Yet she felt certain it was not Jane's voice but Elizabeth's which echoed with frustration.

"I would rather," Mrs Bennet began, speaking patiently to a daughter who must be truly stupid not to already see and agree with her point of view. "I would rather you accept your cousin's proposal and stop bringing shame on the family. Mr Collins is a - a - settled man. He has a home and a profession and one day will inherit Longbourn. If you are his wife there is a chance we may all of us keep our home!"

Mr Collins? And Elizabeth as his wife? The idea struck Mary as so absurd that she could hardly keep from laughing as she drew closer to the three huddled women. This sound alerted them to her presence and her mother and sisters all looked up to see who approached.

"Mary!" Elizabeth cried with relief. "Here, you will take my side, I am sure of it. Mama, listen, you cannot disagree with *three* of your daughters."

Mrs Bennet sniffed, as if to indicate she certainly could, and would, if this daughter persisted in the same nonsense as the other two.

"I must have misunderstood," Mary began, frowning. "I only came to see what had happened, and to check that you were quite well, Lizzy..."

"Well?" Elizabeth laughed, a hollow, bitter sound. "Yes, indeed I am well, if you consider my mother's intent to marry me off to a buffoon."

Mary's heart sank. Then it was true?

"Mr Collins has proposed," Jane said, in a low, calm voice. "Although why he chose to do it here, of all places, is a mystery."

"And in front of everyone!" Lizzy groaned and buried her face in her hands. "I am utterly mortified."

"It is Mr Collins who ought to be embarrassed," Mary said, stoutly. "It was a foolish idea to propose at all, let alone to do it in front of an audience."

"Mary!" Mrs Bennet whirled around on her. "And since when have you become an expert on proposals, pray?"

"I am not," Mary acknowledged. "But I certainly know enough to think they ought to take place quietly, and with some understanding that the recipient is inclined to accept." She turned to Lizzy. "Was it very bad?"

"Awful!" Lizzy said, a slight smile beginning to tug at the edges of her lips. "He talked to me about shelves, and promised that I might choose whatever fabric I desired for a new pair of curtains to celebrate our return to Hunsford as man and wife." She shook her head, vehemently. "Curtains! As if that were all a woman could wish for in her married life."

Mrs Bennet drew her lips together but mercifully said nothing.

"What did you say?" Mary ventured, eager to learn exactly what had happened.

"I was too shocked to say very much of anything!" Lizzy said. "I merely begged him not to say any more, and he ignored me, so when he took a breath to compose himself before mounting a second argument - for his first was met with silence, I can assure you - I pulled my hand free, and fled." The absurdity of the event struck Elizabeth, and her smile returned. "Poor Mr Collins. But honestly, it is rather a ridiculous notion, our marrying at all. And to ask me here! Now!" She shook her head.

"I think it demonstrates his courage," Mrs Bennet said, stoutly. "His courage and the depth of his affection for you, Lizzy. I am sure your refusal has wounded him deeply."

"Wounded his pride, perhaps." Lizzy conceded. "But as he is blessed with so much of it, I am sure it will not be too much of a problem for him."

"Elizabeth!" Mrs Bennet was shocked to hear Lizzy's candid words. "I am very unhappy with this turn of affairs. Very unhappy!" She folded her arms across her front, and drooped, like a plant in need of water.

"And I am sorry for it, Mama, but you cannot expect me to marry such a man."

"Such a man will save your family!" Mrs Bennet pressed. "And surely he cannot be so very bad. He is our cousin- "

"Who we hardly knew of before his arrival this winter!"

"But -"

Mary watched her mother's forehead crease into a frown of concentration. She could tell her mother was busily scheming, trying to find some angle with which she could appeal to Lizzy's better nature and somehow convince her to change her position. *It will not work, Mama*, she tried to communicate in silence. *Lizzy is too strong, too forthright to ever agree to such a match.* She did not permit herself to think how disappointed she was that her mother would pursue the idea, knowing how much her eldest daughter despaired of it. Would she truly rather Lizzy be miserable, married to a man she did not respect or even like, simply because it guaranteed the Bennet family's claim to Longbourn? Mary very much feared she would, and was disappointed to acknowledge her mother's mercenary nature.

"You must accept him, Lizzy," Mrs Bennet began again, relaxing her pose into one of comfort. She reached for her daughter and tried to draw Elizabeth to her in an embrace. "I know it may not be what you may wish for now, but you shall see. People change. Once you are married, you will begin to appreciate Mr Collins all the more. He is - he is a *kind* man, and that is something even you cannot dispute. Kind, yes, and good. Why, he must be, if he is a curate!" She laughed, attempting to lighten the atmosphere. "I am sure, once you come to know him better you will learn still more to care for him, and at last, maybe even love him."

"I shall never!" Elizabeth cried, swerving out of her mother's arms. "Mama, I have made my position perfectly clear. How can you try to continue to try to convince me otherwise? I have refused Mr Collins. If he is foolish enough to ask me again, I shall refuse him again. I certainly will never marry the man, no matter what you say to persuade me."

"Oh?"

With one word, Mrs Bennet's attitude shifted. She straightened, her compassionate smile turning into something that was almost a scowl.

"Well, if you refuse to marry him, then I certainly cannot ever imagine you marrying anyone. I wash my hands of you, Elizabeth. If you wish to be a poor spinster and miserable all the rest of your days, then you must do as you see fit. Certainly, you do not care one whit for your poor mother, or your sisters, if you will not put their own needs - yes, I use the word needs - above your own desire for perfection. You will soon learn, my headstrong girl, that happiness in marriage is an illusion. A woman must make the best choice she can, and be content. True love is fit only for novels."

With a huff, Mrs Bennet pushed past Mary, and returned to the parlour, leaving her three eldest daughters in a state of shocked silence.

"THERE, NOW," RICHARD remarked, as the door opened to permit Mrs Bennet. "Their mother returns, so all cannot be so very dreadful."

Darcy nodded, and returned, half-heartedly to the comment he had been making.

"I cannot imagine our aunt delights at your delay."

"She does not mind it," Richard said, with a grin. "For she thinks I will somehow induce you to accompany me."

Darcy made a noise somewhere between a cough and a snort that perfectly conveyed his disapproval of this suggestion.

Richard opened his mouth to speak again, but Mrs Bennet had reached Mr Collins' side and spoke in a stage-whisper pointed enough that it carried to the cousins' ears, and both gentlemen heard it, whether they wished to or not.

"You must not be discouraged, Mr Collins," Mrs Bennet whispered. "Many young ladies refuse at first, especially to an offer so sudden and so surprising as yours was to poor Lizzy. Truly, I say to you it is out of her meekness, her good character and the natural shyness befitting a young lady like my daughter that she refused you. You must rally, and try again -"

Richard felt a flicker of laughter bubble in the back of his throat, and turned away, lest the sound carry. He noticed his cousin's dark eyes were darker still, shooting daggers at the couple who were still in deep discussion of the apparent shyness of Elizabeth Bennet. Richard could not believe Collins gullible enough to buy such an explanation. Elizabeth Bennet did not seem to him the least bit shy: quite the opposite in fact. She knew her own mind and was unafraid of exercising her true and certain will. She would make a dreadful wife for a buffoon such as Collins. Apparently, Darcy shared his opinion, for he spoke again, in a voice so low that Richard had to stoop to catch his words.

"So he proposed. No wonder Miss Elizabeth felt the need to flee."

Richard nodded but said nothing, sure that any sound he might make would jolt Darcy back to full consciousness and prevent him from speaking what was truly on his mind. Instead, he made an impression of staring out of the window into the blackness, allowing his cousin to merely wonder aloud.

"The idea is absurd, utterly so. I declare I would marry her myself before condemning her to such a match."

This remark was so surprising to Richard that his gaze darted back to Darcy and his attempts at immovability were forgotten.

So my suspicions were correct. Darcy does care for Elizabeth Bennet, at least far more than he might own in his right mind. His offer is a magnanimous one, but I wager it springs from real feeling and not any other sense of duty. My cousin has a good heart but he is no Samaritan, and marriage is far more than any man's Christian duty.

Wondering if Darcy was aware he had spoken his thoughts aloud, and thus betrayed himself, Richard weighed his response carefully. Nonchalance was decided to be his best option, and when he spoke it was with a calculated lightness.

"I do not like the curate's chances of securing a different answer if he is foolishness to pose the question again."

"He is foolish to take his advice from Mrs Bennet, who seems willfully blind to the true nature of her daughter. Meekness? Miss Elizabeth has many admiral qualities, but I could not charge her with shyness if my life depended on it."

"She merely wishes to see her daughters married," Richard said, calmly. "Is that so bad a desire?"

"She merely wishes to secure her own future," Darcy responded, his eyes flashing with anger. "Longbourn will go to Collins in the fullness of time, if she can secure him by marriage to one of her own daughters she may keep her home."

Richard's features quirked with good humour.

"In that, she is not unlike a beloved relative of our own."

Darcy glanced up, frowning as he processed his cousin's words.

"Aunt Catherine is not a martyr in her desire to match you and Anne. She has her reasons. She has far less interest in my own affairs, but then my fortune is modest indeed, in comparison with Pemberley."

"I care little for fortune -"

"That is because you possess it." Richard shrugged his shoulders. "I am aware of my own advantages and do not despise the small amount I have accrued through inheritance and my own efforts. It will secure a modest home for myself and my wife, when I secure her." He smiled, enigmatically, not yet ready to be as open with his cousin as Darcy had unwittingly been with him on the nature of his affections. "On reflection, I rather think I ought to rejoice in the smallness of it, for it allows me to live my life as I see fit. Any more, and so many people would take an interest in my decisions that it might make life very constraining indeed."

"Am I so constrained?" Darcy grumbled.

"You feel pursued into a marriage you do not desire, and here fate provides you with a simple way out."

Richard did not wish to spell the scheme out, when Darcy had made mention of it himself just moments before. He watched his cousin's face carefully, seeing a light come into his eyes that indicated he understood Richard's meaning just as well.

"Really, cousin," he remarked, with a lift of his chin. "You speak utter nonsense at times. I wager you have had your fill of brandy this evening. Come, let us go and speak to Charles. The poor fellow looks utterly lost in Miss Bennet's absence. I do not think there will be any more dancing this evening."

Richard nodded, and fell into step beside his cousin, content that with but one or two small pushes more, Darcy might be manoeuvred into the position he, Richard, knew he wished to take. It would take some skill to ensure that Darcy did not feel any effort other than his own, for he railed at the thought of manipulation, and Richard did not wish to trick his cousin, even if he felt certain that marriage to Elizabeth Bennet might be the very thing his cousin needed, whether he quite knew it yet or not.

As for my own heart, Richard thought, with a cursory glance towards the door that Mary had departed through in search of her sister. *I will be patient and bide my time.* He glanced at Collins as he passed, and a few words from Mrs Bennet reached his ears that made the blood flash in his veins.

"...and if not Lizzy, well! My dear Mr Collins, I have three younger daughters who would, I am sure, suit you just as well!"

I might bide my time but must not take too long before I speak. He did not think Mary strong enough to resist the influence of both her cousin and her mother, if she was placed in a corner. And for some reason he could not quite fathom he very much wished her to choose him for himself, and not because he offered her an escape from a worse fate.

Chapter Twelve

"Well, Lizzy, the weather is certainly fine enough to allow for a visit to Meryton. Jane and Mary will accompany you?" Mr Bennet spoke cheerily, as if there were nothing at all unusual about taking breakfast in utter silence. His comment was met with a few polite murmurs from his three elder daughters, and the table lapsed once more into awkward quiet.

"Do Miss Kitty and Miss Lydia not intend on joining you in Meryton, Miss Elizabeth?" Mr Collins asked, putting a simpering inflexion over her name.

"You would have to ask them that, sir," Elizabeth replied sweetly, before turning deliberately to Jane and attempting to engage her in conversation.

Mrs Bennet sniffed loudly, and Lizzy glanced momentarily towards her mother.

"Do you have a cold, Mama?"

"My health is the least of my concerns at present!" Mrs Bennet cried. She sniffed still louder, shooting Elizabeth an angry glance, before very pointedly turning away.

Well, there is some small improvement at least, Elizabeth thought, with a wry smile. *Mama is speaking to me.* Since Mr Collins' disastrous refusal last evening, Mrs Bennet had not said a word to Elizabeth, but had insisted on being often near her, so that her daughter might experience the full depth of her annoyance. Her campaign of silence, now broken, appeared ended almost entirely.

"Perhaps Mr Collins will be kind enough to accompany you to Meryton," she ventured.

"I am quite sure Mr Collins has better things to do with his time," Jane said, swiftly forestalling the argument she could sense brewing. "And in any case, Colonel Fitzwilliam and Mr Darcy have already agreed to escort us."

"Oh." Mrs Bennet's features fell. "Does not Mr Bingley come with them? And his sister? Now they are a charming pair I do so wish you to be friends with, Jane..."

Excluding Elizabeth once more from her conversation and her notice, Mrs Bennet fixed her attention on her eldest daughter, heaping praise on her for her choice of beau and general good-nature. "If only each of my daughters could be so good as you are, dear Jane!"

Lizzy rolled her eyes towards the ceiling, and turned towards Lydia and Kitty, who were dozing in one corner of the table.

"What are your plans for the day?" She asked, determined that she would no longer be confined to silence and seeking any conversation that might keep her safe from Mr Collins' attention.

"Sleep!" Kitty yawned.

"Yes, for you and Jane will have a dull trip to Meryton planned, if I am not mistaken. I do not even imagine you intend to call on the regiment..."

"In that case you are correct," Elizabeth said, unduly relieved that her morning would not be spoilt by wrangling her younger sisters. "Although I believe Colonel Fitzwilliam intends on calling on them. I do not imagine we shall stay long, though, for he also has a desire to purchase some music." Her eyes flickered to Mary. "And so we are taking our resident songbird with us for advice."

"Mary?" Lydia asked, scornfully. "And what does she know of fashionable pieces? You only play the airs and jigs we like when we beg you, everything you prefer is so dreary!"

"Not all music is designed for dancing," Mary countered, quietly.

"More's the pity!" Kitty observed. "For I do not think music worth a single consideration if one cannot dance to it."

"That is because you cannot play," Mary replied, lifting her chin. "Your singing is dreadful and I very much wonder if you could detect a tune if it were presented to you on a plate."

Elizabeth could scarcely prevent an amused smile from creeping across her face. *Well done, Mary!* She thought, surprised and pleased to see her sister holding her own where before she would have simply sunk lower into her seat and worn whatever criticism her sisters thought up to throw at her. Something was different in Mary, although Elizabeth could not quite put her finger on it. She sat a little straighter, her features were a fraction more relaxed. It was almost as if she were more aware of herself, and less willing to shrink at the first hint of a slight.

"Colonel Fitzwilliam certainly seemed happy enough with Mary's choices of music on the occasions he has heard her play,"

Elizabeth confirmed. "So perhaps he *wishes* for music that is a little different to the airs and jigs you are so insistent on, Kitty."

Her younger sister pouted, and returned to her meal, but Mary shot her a grateful smile, and the sisters shared a moment of silent affection in the midst of the chilly silence that once more descended over the breakfast table.

"Mr Collins," Mr Bennet announced, with great effort. "Perhaps you would give me the honour of your presence in my study this morning. There are a few matters of business I wish to discuss with a...ah...a gentlemanly mind, such as your own."

Mrs Bennet turned almost purple with irritation at her husband's insistence in undercutting her plans. She, Lizzy felt certain, had intended on Mr Collins' accompanying them, by accident or design, to Meryton, and somehow being afforded the opportunity to state his desire once more to marry Elizabeth. How this would work out in his favour, Lizzy was at a loss to understand, for Mr Collins would appear still less desirable in company with three intelligent, handsome gentlemen such as Mr Bingley, Mr Darcy and Colonel Fitzwilliam. This idea brought another smile to Elizabeth's features as she was forced to acknowledge, not for the first time, that in comparison to Mr Collins even Mr Darcy was a desirable gentleman. In fact, Elizabeth was forced to realise that even without Mr Collins to offer so damning an alternative, Mr Darcy would not be so terrible a prospect. This suggestion caught in Elizabeth's throat, and she coughed, suddenly, drawing the attention of her mother.

"Oh, Lizzy! Must you always find reasons to laugh at things that are not remotely amusing?" She threw down her napkin and marched out of the room, which allowed all of its occupants to let out a hushed sigh of relief.

At last, I must admit Mama is correct! Elizabeth thought to herself, pushing the remainder of her food around on the plate, her appetite gone. *The idea of finding Mr Darcy a good prospect for marriage - for my own marriage! - with or without Mr Collins to offer an alternative is not amusing in the least...*

IT WAS STILL RELATIVELY early when three gentlemen's horses were recognised on their approach to Longbourn.

"Here they are!" Jane cried, happily, as she, Lizzy and Mary hurried out to meet them.

Mary felt a flicker of nervousness, but Lizzy grabbed her hand and pulled her alongside her before she was able to devise a reason to escape the visit.

"Ladies!" Mr Bingley said, dismounting from his horse quickly and hurrying forward with an exuberant bow. "How elegant you all look."

"You are too kind, Mr Bingley!" Jane said.

"And too generous!" Lizzy called. "All of us could do with an hour's additional sleep after last night's entertainments, but nonetheless we will thank you for your compliment."

Everybody laughed, although Mary's was awkward and forced. She was intrigued to see Mr Darcy, too, appeared merely to grimace rather than actually to laugh and wondered at how different his manner was to his cousin. Colonel Fitzwilliam followed suit after Mr Bingley and clambered off his horse, in order to greet the ladies with a polite bow. Mr Darcy joined the group with his feet on the ground last of all, and after a polite bow that was almost as stilted as his laugh had been, he asked where they might stable their horses for the afternoon.

"That is, if you ladies remain content to walk?"

"Certainly we do!" Lizzy said. "Meryton is but a mile and I, for one, am eager for the exercise."

Her easy smile fell fractionally when there was a noise from within the house, and Mrs Bennet's voice could be heard declaring,

"I do not see why I must wave them off, Mr Bennet. Lizzy is so contrary and disobedient that I might happily not have her for a daughter at all!"

Mary was shocked to hear her mother speak so, and further embarrassed that her voice must have carried enough that the gentlemen all heard. Lizzy's face flamed with colour, and, wanting to spare her sister any embarrassment she could, Mary threw herself into the breach, her nerves forgotten in her desire to aid her sister.

"Colonel Fitzwilliam," she said, desperately. "Have you - have you seen much of Meryton since your arrival in Hertfordshire?"

"I have not, Miss Mary." He smiled, and seemed utterly delighted to be drawn into a conversation about the merits and flaws of their nearest town, which Mary found herself discussing with more enthusiasm than she ever had before.

There was another sound from within, and at last, the door opened to permit Mr Bennet, who looked bemused by the pretty tableaux unfolding before him.

"Good morning, gentlemen!" he said, with cheer. "Colonel Fitzwilliam, I thought I heard your voice. How are you, sir?"

Mary smiled to see her father singling out Colonel Fitzwilliam. Of the three, she understood he was the least well-positioned and certainly the least wealthy, yet with a few words his father had elevated his position to one of welcome, suggesting the two were far closer friends than Mr Bennet was with either Mr Bingley or Mr Darcy.

"Quite well, thank you, and all the better for our plan to walk to Meryton," Colonel Fitzwilliam said with a grin. "Your daughter has just been informing me of all the delights that await us."

"Indeed!" Mr Bennet laughed. "Well, I should not allow my hopes to soar too high if I were you. Meryton is pleasant enough, but beyond hair ribbons and tea, and that infernal regiment - no offence intended to you, sir, whose rank and record speak for themselves - Meryton is hardly a place I seek to spend any more time than I must."

"You are wise to say so, Mr Bennet," Colonel Fitzwilliam continued. "And I do not doubt if I had a study as fine as yours in which to spend my time I should be of the same opinion."

Mary was surprised to see the effect this warm compliment had upon her father, whose eyes twinkled, until he threw back his head and laughed.

"Well, you are welcome to join me in it should you wish to after your trip." As if suddenly recalling the rest of their party, Mr Bennet waved his hand over the other young men present. "Mr Bingley, Mr Darcy, you are of course also welcome to call upon your return. I do not doubt my women-folk will be eager to see you." He paused. "It is still rather early for the more delicate of my daughters, and my dear wife. Her head aches..." He trailed off, as if this were explanation enough for

Mrs Bennet's poor manners and even poorer commentary on the arrivals.

"Oh dear!" Mr Bingley was concerned. "Ought we not to have come so early?"

"It is of no consequence!" Mr Bennet waved away his comment. "And as you can see, the three ladies you desired to take with you are all happy to be taken!" He smiled. "I do not doubt the quiet will afford rest to those of us that require it." His gaze met Elizabeth's with a gentle smile, and Mary felt a flash of affection for her father. Clearly, he agreed with her and Jane that Elizabeth was acting as she must, to avoid a marriage to a man she disliked. It was only Mama who was so stubbornly wedded to the idea. "Are these your horses? Fine animals. Come, I shall call my groom..."

Mr Darcy and Mr Bingley took the horses after Mr Bennet, leaving Colonel Fitzwilliam and the three ladies to wait for their return.

"Miss Elizabeth," Colonel Fitzwilliam said, after a moment. "I do hope you are recovered after last evening. My cousin, in particular, was concerned for your health."

"Your cousin?" Elizabeth's eyebrows lifted. "Mr Darcy?"

Something approaching a smile flickered across her face, but soon collapsed in favour of a hard frown.

"I am sure he had no end of comments to make on the poor character demonstrated by my behaviour. It was merely the heat and exertion, for I had danced too often without a rest. Please do assure him that I am quite, quite well this morning."

"You may assure him yourself!" Colonel Fitzwilliam said. "For here he comes. Shall we begin our walk?"

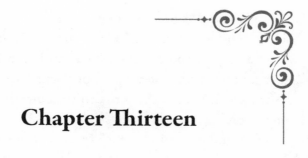

Chapter Thirteen

It was more by chance than design that Richard found himself walking beside Mary towards Meryton. He had, of course, fully intended to design it if necessary but by happy coincidence, Mr Bingley and Jane walked with determination at the head of the group, and Elizabeth, in desiring to speak with them walked after them. Darcy had let out one short sigh but then fallen into step beside her, and the four were engaged in a lively conversation of which Richard could hear only the occasional word or phrase. He happily accompanied Mary, and she continued to speak of the delights of Meryton as if it were quite unlike any other town in all of England. A slow smile crept over his face as he deduced, correctly, that it was anxiety rather than any personal enthusiasm for Meryton that gave energy to her words, and he allowed her to run on for some minutes before she paused for breath and evidently struggled to think of any more to say.

"Well, Miss Mary! That is a very thorough account of what lies before us in Meryton."

"Oh!" She smiled. "Well, it gives a little idea at least. I imagine you have seen many more interesting places on your travels."

"Yes, if you count mountains and the backs of other soldiers' heads as interesting." He laughed. "I am sure Meryton will be a very welcome change, for I was last in London and am eager for a little quieter pace of living before I move on to Kent which is, I am afraid to confess, quite deadly quiet by comparison."

"I have never been to Kent," Mary said, shyly. "Although I have on occasion visited London. My aunt and uncle live there."

"Oh?" He hoped she might take his question for a prompt and offer some description of her relatives and what part of London they resided in, that he could see if they had any connections in common. She merely nodded, and he was compelled to ask the question outright.

"And what part of London do this aunt and uncle Bennet live?"

"Gardiner," Mary corrected. "Their name is Gardiner. And they live -" she darted a glance up the road towards her sisters and looked back at him as if daring a challenge. "They live in Gracechurch Street."

Richard ran through his knowledge of London society and understood, almost immediately, the motive for her glance towards her sisters. Gracechurch Street was not the most elegant part of the city. In fact, Richard had been there often, although naturally without his own cousin's company.

"I know it well," he said, smoothly. After a moment's silence, he ventured to speak a little more. "If I may be so brave, Miss Mary, I must invite you not to draw a direct comparison between my cousin and I. I value Darcy highly, we are cousins after all and have been good friends all our lives, but our lives and our circumstances are quite different."

Mary looked at him, curiously.

"I am not as wealthy as he, nor possess the properties he does. As you may have gathered by my title, it was down to me to earn my fortune, and I have, albeit a modest one, by comparison to my two friends up yonder."

"You speak as if that were something to be ashamed of!"

"It is not - and I am not, but I am eager that you understand my circumstances, because -"

"Mr Darcy?"

The shout from some distance down the street caught Richard's ear and prevented him from finishing his words, but before he had time to rue the stranger who disturbed them, he saw his cousin's back stiffen.

"It cannot be -" Bingley muttered.

Darcy glanced over his shoulder, and Richard understood the look in a moment. As the man drew nearer he recognised him, and his own blood began to boil. George Wickham. He had heard the man was in Meryton but never dreamed their paths might cross.

"Good morning! What a party you are!"

"Good morning," Darcy replied, stiffly. "I see you are alone."

"Will you not introduce me to your friends?" Wickham asked, with a smile as he watched Darcy uncomfortably acquiesce to his manners.

"Mr George Wickham, this is Miss Jane Bennet, Miss Elizabeth and Miss Mary Bennet."

"Delighted," Wickham said, with a deep bow.

"And you remember Charles Bingley and my cousin, Colonel Fitzwilliam."

Darcy had put an emphasis on Richard's title and he, like his cousin, was gratified to see Wickham flinch, his expression dropping almost imperceptibly.

"Colonel Fitzwilliam." Wickham nodded. "It has been quite some time."

"Indeed it has, Mr Wickham. I hear that you are part of the regiment here at Meryton." He fixed him with a glare. "That is headed by Colonel Forster, is it not?"

"That's right."

"He is a good man. I am well acquainted with him."

"Oh?"

Richard could see the sheen of desperation that settled over Wickham's forehead.

"Well, I will not delay you further, gentlemen," he said, with a hurried bow. "Good morning, ladies."

The party stood to one side to allow Wickham to pass, and Richard could almost have laughed to see the careful way he continued on his path. How it contrasted with the jaunty way he had approached, determined to undermine Darcy's happiness and instead having his own precarious position rendered still more unsteady by Richard's presence. He still intended to alert Colonel Foster to the past behaviour of his newest recruit. There would be no mentioning of names, no detail, merely an acknowledgement that their paths had crossed, and a suggestion that Forster keep a tight watch on Wickham, for the man had a reputation as a scoundrel. It would not undo the damage he had wrought on poor Georgiana, or on Darcy, who had been bound by honour and by old Mr Darcy's promise of care to see Wickham well, but it might encourage the man to keep his head down and behave better in future. Richard sighed. He doubted Wickham would be capable of behaving well in future. How many opportunities had he already had for learning his lesson, and yet he persisted?

"I did not realise you had other friends in Meryton, Colonel Fitzwilliam," Mary said, shyly. "I fear you surprised him by your presence."

"I fear I did!" Colonel Fitzwilliam asserted, as the party began to walk once more. "And I further wager he was not as happy to see me as a true friend might have been. But Wickham is scarcely worth our conversation, Miss Mary. Come, I wish to hear more of music. You recall my complete illiteracy when it comes to compositions. I do hope to impress my aunt and cousin upon my visit to Rosings, so perhaps you would be kind enough to educate me. What was the piece that Miss Bingley played last evening, for instance, when we danced? It was not so fast, nor so technically difficult, I am sure, as the pieces you chose."

This gentle compliment caused Mary's whole face to light up, and Richard scoured his memory for more he could say in praise of Mary's musical accomplishments, for it was not even a falsehood on his part to admire her playing. Truly she was talented, and he had sought to take an interest in music he had never had before in hopes he might have reason to use his newfound knowledge and please her.

Mary chattered happily about the pieces, both her own and those that Caroline had played, how they were suited for dancing because of their lively pace and the easily followed beats that instructed, without the need of words, the dancers when to move.

"I see it is strategy, at its finest," he marvelled, with a grin, and dropped his voice. "For do not think I did not notice the slow, romantic piece you played the first time your sister and Mr Bingley danced. You would play your part in encouraging a particular style of dance, of conversation between partners by your choice of music."

Mary's cheeks flamed.

"I would not say that -"

"Such modesty. Yet you certainly observe more than you admit to, I am sure. For instance, you understood almost immediately how I would feel coming into so close-knit a society as this after so many months away and have made every effort to see me settled, even when it requires you to speak rather more than you might personally choose." He smiled, warmly. "It is appreciated, Miss Mary. You are a very generous person, and I am glad to call you my friend. At least, I hope I may be so bold as to call you my friend?"

He held his breath, wondering if in her answer Mary might crush the hopes that had begun to lodge with ever more fervency in his chest. His relief was palpable, then, when she murmured, so softly that he might have missed it entirely, had he not had his eyes fixed on her features.

"Yes, Colonel Fitzwilliam. Of course, you may!"

DARCY HAD NOT SAID a word since they passed George Wickham. He could not get the scoundrel's sly smirk out of his mind. He had approached determined to ruin the morning,

he was sure, and it seemed as if he had succeeded. Sensing
Darcy's discomfort with rather more grace than her sister, he
heard Jane Bennet inquire quietly of Bingley "whether that
gentleman was a friend of Mr Darcy's?" To his credit, Bingley
had denied it and claimed the two shared an unhappy past
connection. He went further still, intimating that he, Bingley,
was equally unhappy to know of Wickham's presence in
Meryton, but was determined that such a fellow would not
spoil their walk, and would Miss Bennet not be so kind as to
tell him the name of that tree up ahead with the large green
leaves?

Darcy made a promise to himself that he would thank
Charles later for his efforts, and focused his energy on walking,
with purpose, hoping that with enough force to his steps he
might shed some of the energy he might more gleefully have
turned against Wickham's face, smirk and all.

"I did not realise you knew so many people in
Hertfordshire, Mr Darcy," Elizabeth Bennet asked, after a
moment more of quiet.

"I know many people," he replied, unwilling to be drawn
on the nature of his connection with George Wickham.

"Then I am sorry that the person whose path you crossed
today is not someone you think fondly of," she said, with a
generosity of spirit that compelled him to lift his gaze. He
saw curiosity darkening her features, yes, but something more
beyond. She was sympathetic, concerned that he was not
unduly unsettled by the unhappy meeting. *Concerned for me?*
Darcy felt a tiny flicker of hope, but before he could nurse it
into being Elizabeth spoke again.

"You are kind to accompany my sisters and me to Meryton, Mr Darcy. I am sure you have far more important things to be doing with your time."

"Important?" He lifted one corner of his lips in a half-smile. "Indeed, like haunting Netherfield with none but Miss Bingley and Mrs Hurst for company."

Elizabeth laughed, and he felt sure it was the loveliest sound he had heard that morning, chasing away the spectre of George Wickham into the far recesses of Darcy's mind.

"And what of poor Mr Hurst, is he not company for you?"

"He is hardly company when he is sleeping, which is often." Darcy frowned. "He is hardly energetic company when he is *not* sleeping..."

"And that is what you crave, is it? Energetic company?" Elizabeth's head tilted. "You surprise me, Mr Darcy. I felt certain you preferred silence, but if company is insisted upon then it must also be quiet."

"I confess I prefer calm to chaos, is that worthy of comment?"

"Not at all," Elizabeth said. "On this point, we are not dissimilar, although I wager our means for finding calm differ. You enjoy a solitary seat indoors: I seek it on a walk."

"And so today we must both test your method," Darcy remarked, gesturing to the path before them, occupied by Charles and Jane Bennet.

"Ah, this is but a short journey!" Elizabeth said, with a smile. "One mile only!"

"Indeed, I forgot. A walk is not to be countenanced unless it consists of upwards of three miles, preferably through rain and mud, so that when one reaches one's destination one is not only exhausted, but frozen and filthy to boot."

Elizabeth laughed again, and Darcy determined to recall the nature of their conversation in provoking such a reaction that he might use it again to such effect.

"You tease me, Mr Darcy! And before now I was convinced you did not know how."

"Because I do not do a thing often is not to suggest I am utterly incapable," Darcy said, his voice low and tinged with more urgency than he intended. Suddenly fearing he was in danger of straying too close to things he did not wish to mention, or, worse, betraying his feelings to the very woman he wished to conceal them from until he could better gauge her own, he cleared his throat, and, lifting his gaze, changed the subject. "Is that not Meryton ahead? How quickly we have reached it!"

"Indeed," Elizabeth said, a slight flicker of confusion darting across her features at Darcy's sudden change in attitude.

"You wished to look at music, cousin?" He turned toward Richard, who was at that moment speaking in a low voice to Mary Bennet and did not respond straight away to Darcy's comment. Elizabeth, too, noticed the quiet couple and remarked upon it.

"What a sweet picture they make, Mr Darcy!" She spoke in a whisper, and moved a little closer, that she might be heard only by him. "I do not suppose your cousin anticipated losing his heart on his visit to Hertfordshire?"

"His heart?" Darcy craned his neck to look once more. It was his cousin, right enough, and yet Richard Fitzwilliam looked different than Darcy could ever recall seeing him. There was a gentleness, a kindness to his actions in the way he accompanied the young Miss Bennet, as if he were concerned only for her. His attention was on their conversation, and he nodded, encouraging her to speak and rewarding every word with a smile or a nod as if it were quite the most compelling conversation he had ever been a part of.

"You disapprove?" Elizabeth asked, her voice catching. This time Darcy did not look at her. He could not tear his eyes away from his cousin and Miss Mary, seeing for the first time what Elizabeth and Jane, and probably Charles too, for despite his impression of ignorance, he knew his friend to be far more attuned to the feelings of others than he was often given credit for, had seen with a glance. Richard was happy, more so than Darcy ever recalled seeing him. He might have made his career in the military but this was a man eager for a home of his own, which state Darcy could well understand. It was his cousin's evident desire for a wife - and such a wife - that until now Darcy had not fully appreciated.

"No," he said, softly. "I do not disapprove."

Had Richard formed such an attachment weeks earlier, or perhaps if Darcy had been aware of it only days sooner than he was, he might not have been so content with the suggestion of his cousin aligning himself with a member of the Bennet family. But Darcy was not insensible of the change his own feelings were undergoing.

"I am glad," Elizabeth said, and this time when Darcy did look at her, she smiled, almost wistfully, in his direction.

Darcy's own heart lifted.

Perhaps I must learn from my cousin. Bachelor living is wearing indeed. Would it be such a terrible thing to marry, and to marry such a woman as this?

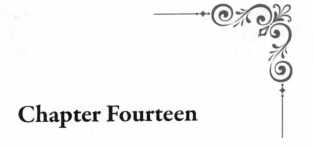

Chapter Fourteen

Meryton was not especially busy, but when they reached their destination it became clear that the small music shop would not comfortably house the entire party.

"There is no problem," Darcy remarked. "Bingley, I wish to enquire about a new pair of gloves. Perhaps we might go directly to the outfitters, and meet the ladies, and you, cousin, for tea?"

This was agreed upon as being the best course of action, although Richard felt a flicker of anxiety at being left to fend for himself amongst all three ladies. He was very soon put at his ease, by Jane's questions pertaining to his aunt and cousin, and Elizabeth's good humour about her own musical abilities. Only Mary was quiet, and at first, Richard worried he had said or done something amiss during the walk to town. He had been pleased to be able to converse so freely and to see her step out of her shell a little. She was quieter than Elizabeth, certainly, but appeared to share her same powers of observation, and had the ability to remark humorously, in so quiet a manner, that he had found the entire journey quite enjoyable. There had been something so natural about the way they had walked and talked that he had begun to hope she might mirror his feelings and afford him the chance to ask the question he dearly wished to ask, yet he still delayed, fearing he would speak to soon and surprise or upset her.

"And what is the piano like at Rosings, Colonel Fitzwilliam?" Jane asked. "We have heard much of Rosings grandness and decor from our cousin -" Here she paused and gave Elizabeth a cautious glance, before continuing. "But, alas, he has not spoken at all of Lady Catherine or her daughter's love of music. I imagine they must have a very beautiful instrument."

"Beautiful, yes," Richard said, running his eyes over the interior of the small shop, and wondering how anybody made sense of the black lines and squiggles that appeared to him like hieroglyphs from an ancient culture. "That is, I imagine so. I believe my aunt has recently purchased a new piano for my cousin to play, so I am afraid I can only speak to their previous instrument which was indeed a fine one."

"How lovely it must be to have a new piano!" Mary remarked, with a faint sigh.

"Ours is unfortunately quite old," Elizabeth said. "And has been hammered on so often by five sets of hands as each of us matured and realised we had very little skill at playing and even less interest in learning - all save Mary, of course, who outshines us all!"

Mary coloured at this praise and turned her attention to a selection of music books on a shelf. She picked one, it seemed to Richard, at random, and handed it to him.

"This might be something your cousin would enjoy, although I fear she may already be familiar with it." She frowned, and Richard felt a flicker of concern at her attempt to please him by finding something new and interesting to recommend to a young lady who was as yet but a name to her.

"What of the piece you were playing that very first day I stumbled into Longbourn?" Richard asked, glancing over the book she had handed him and nodding, though he could not make head nor tails of its contents. "That was a particularly lovely piece, and has quite haunted me ever since." He grinned. "Although you will be pleased to hear I have not made any attempt at playing it myself. I am all too aware of my precarious position as houseguest and fear the wrath of Miss Bingley, were I to risk playing the piano as hamfistedly as I assuredly would, within her hearing."

"Oh!" Mary smiled. "Well, that is something quite new, but I do not believe they will have another copy here, for I had to order it specially. Perhaps -" Her voice faltered. "I mean, your cousin might take my copy, of course, if you would allow me the time to make my own copy."

"You are most generous, Miss Mary!" Richard smiled. "But I would not dream of putting you to such a task. No, indeed, you must keep your music, and we might find something different for Anne. Perhaps you might tell me the name of the piece, though, so I can mention to her how pretty it is."

"It is *The Song of the Lark*," Mary said. "For you recall, the trills on the notes at the beginning - they repeat towards the end - they mimic the lark's call." She hummed a few notes, breaking off only when she realised all three of her companions were regarding her closely, and coughed. "At least, that is the idea. I am sure it is much clearer when played, and played by someone more skilled than I."

"*More skilled than I*, she says, as if she were not the most talented in our whole family!" Elizabeth said, patting her sister warmly on one shoulder.

"As you have already pointed out to Colonel Fitzwilliam that does not account for much," Mary replied, archly, and Richard laughed to see the sisters interacting so comfortably together. He had no close relationship with his brother, and so he valued both Darcy and Georgiana as closely as if they were more than mere cousins. His life had not been lonely, for he had spent much of it in school or in the military, but he could not help but wonder how different his experiences would have been with a brother or sister close enough in age to tease and be teased by.

"Well, Miss Mary, I am indebted to you," Richard said, taking one final glance through the book of music she had selected, and moving towards the proprietor to pay. "Is there anything else you need, while we are here, ladies? Speak now..." His eyes twinkled, merrily, and everyone laughed.

"You are far too generous to us, Colonel Fitzwilliam. We shall be certain to remember it when we order tea!" Elizabeth said, her eyes gleaming.

"It is not often I have opportunity to be generous," he remarked, making his purchase and following the party back out into the bustling Meryton street, for it seemed to him that in the short quarter-hour they had been inside, the crowd without had multiplied. "And I still consider it paying a debt, for without your choice, Miss Mary, I would but utterly lost." He squinted over his shoulder at the music displayed in the window. "It is all Greek to me!"

"Italian," Mary said, with a smile to indicate she, too, was teasing. "But we shall not hold that against you."

"Come, Jane, Mary, let's go ahead to the tea shop. We must try and secure a pleasant table for when Mr Darcy and Mr Bingley join us!" Elizabeth announced, and the three ladies set off at a pace. Richard hung back a little, walking with a relaxed contentment. He was enjoying his morning, and every word he shared with Mary Bennet, or, indeed, with her sisters, convinced him further. This was the type of family he had dreamed of, and if she would consent to be his wife, and he had reason to hope, from the happy way she smiled at him, that she might, he would spend the rest of his days trying to make her happy.

"LIZZY! OH, JANE, MARY, good morning!"

"Charlotte!" Elizabeth's heart filled at the sight of her friend Charlotte Lucas occupying a table with her sister inside the very tea shop they had selected as their appointed meeting place with Mr Darcy and Mr Bingley. Leaving Colonel Fitzwilliam with Jane and Mary to secure a place for them, Lizzy hurried over to greet Charlotte and Maria with a warm embrace.

"It feels an age since I saw you last!" Charlotte cried. "How are you?" Her intelligent eyes passed over Lizzy's shoulder towards Colonel Fitzwilliam, and returned with a questioning smile. "And who is this dashing young man who accompanies your sisters?"

"Oh have you not yet met Colonel Fitzwilliam?" Lizzy asked. "He is Mr Darcy's cousin, if you can believe it."

"His cousin?" Charlotte looked again, an appraising glance that caused her to nod her head approvingly. "Yes, I can see some slight resemblance. I wager he is far friendlier than Mr Darcy, however."

"I do not know," Lizzy said, with a shrug. "Mr Darcy is not so very bad..."

"Lizzy!" Charlotte was all astonishment, and Maria giggled. "Goodness me, how completely your opinion has changed. I must hold tight to the table for support, as such a thing happens so rarely I am quite convinced the earth is shifting beneath me."

Elizabeth swatted her friend playfully on the arm.

"I merely concede I may have been mistaken in my first assessment, that is all. I am not about to marry the man!" Her lips quirked. "Indeed, I have news on that score also."

"Jane is engaged?" Charlotte guessed.

"No," Lizzy shook her head. "Not yet, at any rate. I am sure there will be an announcement before long, for certainly, Mr Bingley is utterly in love with her."

"That much was apparent at the assembly!" Charlotte laughed. "I am pleased, for he and Jane are both so good they deserve their happiness."

There was a wistful note to Charlotte's voice, and Lizzy felt a flicker of compassion for her friend. Charlotte was intelligent and sensible but sadly plain, and despaired of ever securing a husband, lacking the wealth that might cause a less scrupulous gentleman to overlook an occasional flaw in one's visage.

"It seems to me that she is not the only sister of yours to have secured a beau!" Charlotte said, with a nod towards their friends. "Colonel Fitzwilliam has scarcely looked away from Mary for half a minute since your arrival."

"Yes, he seemed instantly smitten with her, and it appears she returns his feelings, although she is so shy I can't help but feel they will need a little more encouragement in finding their happiness." Lizzy's eyes flickered with fun. "I shall not allow poor Mary's shyness to keep Colonel Fitzwilliam away, for having spoken to him a little I find him thoroughly acceptable as a brother-in-law, and his presence seems to temper Mary into a rather more palatable version of herself." She recounted the few conversations they had had that indicated Colonel Fitzwilliam's good character, and friendly and amusing attitude, and both Charlotte and Maria declared him an altogether agreeable addition to the Netherfield party.

"But that is not all!" Lizzy said, darting a glance over her shoulder to ensure she was not yet missed. "Ah, look, Mr Darcy and Mr Bingley have arrived. I must not tarry long. Will you join us?"

Maria seemed eager, but Charlotte shook her head.

"We are about to leave, so hurry and tell me your news, for who knows when we shall meet again, dear! Life is so busy just at present!"

Elizabeth assumed a comical stance.

"I received a certain proposal of my own, just last evening in fact."

"Not Mr Darcy?" Maria asked, her eyes as wide as saucers.

"No!" Lizzy laughed. "Do not be ridiculous - although, I confess had the gentleman in question been Mr Darcy this story would not be quite so mortifying to my own pride to retell. My dear cousin Mr Collins has deigned to make an offer for my hand." She made a not-completely-inaccurate impression of Mr Collin's snide, sneering tone of voice that provoked still more giggles from Maria, and a slight pursed lip from Charlotte that Lizzy took to be her friend attempting not to laugh too heartily at the behaviour of a gentleman they both knew in his absence.

"Miss Elizabeth...might I pose a question...for you see, it has been suggested to me that I might marry, and seeing that your family consists solely of daughters the matter struck me as most sensible...that is to say, I admire you greatly, and feel so great an *affection*..." At last, Charlotte's silence struck Elizabeth as unusual, and she broke off in her retelling to question her on it.

"My dear Charlotte, is something the matter? It is alright to laugh, I give you full permission, although as you can imagine I did not find the adventure at all amusing myself last evening." She shuddered. "To ask at all, and in such a manner - and at Netherfield, in front of our friends!"

"You refused him?" Charlotte asked.

"Yes, indeed I refused him!" Lizzy shook her head. "How could I marry such a man? How could anybody?" She shrugged her shoulders. "Of course Mama is outraged. She scarcely deigns to speak to me, and argues that I must accept my place and marry him, for the sake of the family. Is it not the most nonsensical thing you have ever heard?"

"No."

Charlotte's one-word answer stunned Lizzy to the core, and she quite immediately ceased her amusement, fixing her friend with a curious gaze.

"No?"

"No, I do not think it nonsensical at all. Your mother, and heed me, Lizzy, for I do not often say this, is eminently sensible on this occasion."

"Sensible?" Lizzy was shocked. "Mama? Charlotte, dear, I do not think you quite understood my tale. Mama is eager that I *accept* Mr Collins -"

"And she is right to be!" Charlotte insisted. "Lizzy, you might think him a buffoon, but he is offering you a home, and a future. Admittedly he may not be as wealthy as...but in any case, you are one of five sisters, what right do you have to be choosy?"

Elizabeth's mouth dropped open in surprise. She could not believe the words that were coming from her friend's lips.

"I know you have always insisted on only marrying for love -"

"As have you!"

"Yes, but I am old enough by now to know that love is only fit for storybooks. In our present time, a young lady must be practical. Marrying Mr Collins will not only secure your future, Lizzy, but your family's beside. In refusing him, you are being...well, I hate to say it, for I love you almost as if you were my own sister, but Lizzy, refusing Mr Collins simply because you do not like him is very selfish of you."

Lizzy could not believe her ears.

"There, now, I am done lecturing." Charlotte at least had the grace to look a little embarrassed to have spoken so harshly to her friend. "I am sorry, I did not mean to speak so plainly, but time is of the essence. I only hope you might still be able to undo the damage. Perhaps if you apologise to Mr Collins, and explain how much his proposal took you by surprise..." She threw up her hands. "I do not know how you might manage it, but I imagine it is not an impossible task. There, Lizzy, your sister is waving. We have kept you too long away from your family. Do, do give my love to Jane and Mary, both. Maria, we are already late to meet Father. Come, let us hurry!"

In one short moment, Charlotte and Maria left the tea room, and in a daze, Lizzy returned to her group.

"How was Charlotte?" Jane asked.

"What a pity you could not convince your friends to join us," Mr Bingley said. "There is quite room enough for all of us here. Now, let us order some tea."

The conversation continued around Elizabeth, but she was half in a daze, and heard none of it.

Selfish? Did Charlotte think her selfish for refusing Mr Collins? She did not see the absurdity of his proposal, or the impossibility of a match between them, but instead seemed surprised that Lizzy could contemplate any course of action other than marrying him, when the very notion seemed the impossible thing to Elizabeth herself.

Ought I to heed Charlotte? To heed Mama? She frowned, turning the idea over in her mind. *Surely I am my own best guide? Surely I must follow my heart?*

"Lizzy?" At last Mary's voice broke through the chaos of Elizabeth's thoughts and recalled her to herself. "Is something the matter?"

"No," Lizzy said, forcing her features into a smile. Her own romantic life might be a disaster, but here she was faced with not one but two sisters who might make truly happy matches. She would do better to think upon that, for now, and puzzle out the problem of Mr Collins later. She lifted her eyes to the rest of the party, and was surprised to see a concerned glance darkening Mr Darcy's face, but it vanished almost as soon as she recognised it.

Chapter Fifteen

Mary had been enjoying the day far more than she expected to. She was delighted to be able to help Colonel Fitzwilliam in his task, and still more delighted to find him eager to talk to her even once the task was completed. She had feared him attentive only insofar as he wanted her help, but no, it seemed he truly wished to converse with her - *her!* - even more than her sisters, although he was all politeness in addressing his remarks to both Jane and her, in Elizabeth's absence. When Mr Bingley arrived, and claimed Jane's attention almost entirely for his own, Colonel Fitzwilliam had turned to Mary with still more energy, quizzing her on her interest in books and travel, enquiring as to whether she had ever been to the north of the country.

"Mr Darcy's estate at Pemberley is grand indeed," he said, with a glance towards his cousin. Mr Darcy did not respond nor, Mary considered, did he even hear Richard's comment. His focus was on his tea, just as it had been on Elizabeth, when she was still speaking to Charlotte. Mary missed her own cue in the conversation out of concern for her sister, who was equally as quiet as Mr Darcy. It was a stranger effect on Elizabeth, however, and Mary was curious as to what Charlotte had said to upset her sister so, for it must be something important to cause Elizabeth to withdraw into herself in such a manner.

"Kent, too, is quite beautiful country...although I am sure you have already heard much of my aunt's estate at Rosings from the lips of your cousin, Mr Collins."

This produced a reaction which startled Mary, for at the mention of "Mr Collins", Elizabeth flinched, and lifted her eyes to the Colonel, looking momentarily like an animal caught in a trap.

"Forgive me, Miss Mary, I am quite sure I tire you with my talk of grand houses," Colonel Fitzwilliam said, with a slight tone to his voice. "No doubt it is mere misdirection on my part, for I am as yet without a home of my own, and must only admire those I am familiar with as from a distance."

Mary turned back to him, all apology.

"No! It is interesting to me." She smiled. "I like to hear you talk, I am sorry for not seeming so." She lifted her tea to her lips. "Please do continue."

Thus encouraged, Colonel Fitzwilliam spoke more of Kent, although Mary noticed that, unlike Mr Collins, who was fixed on describing the wealth and elegance of his patroness's home, her new friend was eager to speak to the history of the place. He mentioned funny stories from the past, referring to scrapes he and Darcy had got into as children, which made Mary laugh and turn to Elizabeth, certain that she would appreciate the joke and still more so because it reflected a carefree side to Mr Darcy that neither sister was remotely familiar with.

"Darcy?" Colonel Fitzwilliam prompted. "I'm quite surprised you have permitted me to go so far in this tale without censure. Or are you waiting until we are alone?" He cringed, comically, and at last Mr Darcy looked up at him, momentary annoyance relaxing into an affectionate, enduring, half-smile.

"I have learnt by now there is little point in stopping you once you are started. Besides, I am sure I can trust the Miss Bennets not to spread rumours of my childish misbehaviour far and wide."

He, too, looked at Elizabeth as if he expected some response, but, again, there was none. Mary laid a hand on her sister's arm, and Lizzy jerked up, spilling her tea.

"Oh! Mary!" she cried, snatching her hand away and brushing at her dress. "You startled me!"

Mary darted back as if she had been struck.

"I'm sorry!" she muttered.

"Now look what you've done!" Elizabeth continued. "My dress is ruined!"

"Not ruined, surely," Jane began in a placating tone.

Mary heard no more, she stood and excused herself, hurrying towards the kitchen ostensibly in search of a cloth but really to afford her the opportunity to hide her face for a moment from the eyes of her friends. It had been a simple error, she knew, and logically she had done nothing to deserve Elizabeth's response, but still, it stung, just when she thought she and her sister were, at last, becoming close.

She drew in a ragged breath, and readied herself to return, but not before a familiar male voice reached her ears.

"Yes, please, a cloth and some water for our table," Colonel Fitzwilliam's voice sounded distracted. "And can you tell me if

a young lady has come this way? She seemed a little upset and
-"

"No young lady, sir. Which table was it?" The tired voice of
their over-burdened hostess cut Colonel Fitzwilliam off before
he could say any more, and Mary sank with relief into the
shadows. Now that the moment was over, she felt silly for
running away. Of course, Elizabeth had meant nothing by her
comment, it was merely surprise, and disappointment at
spilling tea on a favoured dress. Mary, as usual, had misread the
situation and acted unnecessarily. She scoured the hallway to
see if she could find some reason for her absence that she could
hide behind. A fresh pot of milk, perhaps? Or a clean teacup
for Elizabeth? Before she could settle on her request to the
kitchen, the sound of a gentleman clearing his throat startled
her back to the presence.

"Miss Mary! I was worried you had run all the way back
to Longbourn unaccompanied." Colonel Fitzwilliam smiled
gently at her, and Mary felt her anxieties melt away. "Do come
back to our table, for I have not told you the worst of Darcy's
trouble making yet, and you are by far my most attentive
listener."

TEA WAS FINISHED QUITE soon after that, and the party
began their journey back towards Longbourn, albeit in a rather
more sombre mood. Elizabeth seemed determined to walk
alone, and so Darcy fell into step with his cousin and Miss
Mary, a little mollified to be afforded the opportunity to
observe the pair together once more and see if his earlier
deduction was correct.

He felt some responsibility for his cousin, and wondered idly if he ought to take Richard aside and advise him on the path he seemed set on taking, yet something stilled his hand.

What do I know of marriage, that I might advise him? What do I know of proposals?

"And your cousin, Colonel Fitzwilliam," Mary said. "The one you bought the music for. What is she like?"

"Anne?" Richard glanced at Darcy before continuing. "She is not unlike you in temperament, I wager, for she is quiet, and not fond of discord."

They shared a glance that Darcy could not begin to understand, but he let it pass, seeing it as some evidence that his cousin's affections were not in vain. Mary may not be effusive, but it seemed apparent that she did not *dis*like Richard. In fact, she seemed abler and willing to speak with him around than Darcy had ever noticed prior.

"She is paler in colouring than either you or Miss Elizabeth," he offered, feeling as if he ought to contribute at least a word or two to this conversation, being as it concerned a person only he and Richard knew well. "Paler even than Jane, I wager, for her complexion has not the healthy glow afforded by life in the country."

Mary paused a moment.

"Is Kent so different to Hertfordshire?"

"Not in the least!" Richard smiled. "You misunderstand my cousin. Kent has countryside too, and plenty of it. Many a pretty walk and view surround Rosings. But Anne..." He lowered his voice, as if out of respect for the invalid who was a clear county away and unlikely to be disturbed by being thus discussed. "Anne suffers rather a lot with ill health, and as such is not often out of doors."

"Oh dear!" Mary seemed utterly concerned, in a way that surprised and pleased Darcy. She was utterly without artifice, although not so able as her sister to hide her feelings when politeness required it. He thought back to her sudden disappearance at tea and wondered if this, too, had been Mary's only way of managing without breaking down in public. He felt a flare of sympathy, for he, too, did not hide his feelings well, or rather it took a great deal of his energy to do so in a public setting, which was half the reason he so despised public settings! "Oh, Colonel Fitzwilliam, you ought to visit her soon if she is so unwell. Perhaps she might appreciate some cut flowers - there are a few still blooming in our garden, you might take them today -?"

"I see you plan to dispatch me immediately!" Richard laughed, but Darcy understood his cousin well enough to detect a trace of anxiety behind his good humour. "Have I outstayed my welcome in Hertfordshire already?"

"No!" Mary said, her concern becoming worry. "You are very welcome here. That is, we are very grateful you are here. All of us. Mr Darcy -" She glanced at him, in desperation. "I am sure Mr Darcy is very pleased to have you staying with him."

"Indeed I am," Darcy said. "And I believe Miss Mary echoes our sentiments in that we none of us wish you to leave straight away." He winked at his cousin, certain that the gesture went unnoticed by Mary, who had dropped her eyes to the ground. "Anne was doing well, from Aunt Catherine's last report. I am sure they can muddle on without you for another few days at least."

"Then it is decided," Richard said, beaming at Darcy, and taking on a jaunty step as he walked. "I will not depart immediately, and your flowers might bloom a little longer in the ground."

Mary laughed, uncertainly.

Sensing the pair would speak more freely without an audience, Darcy nodded at them both and allowed his pace to slow and draw level with Elizabeth, who was walking with purpose, if not a great deal of energy. Her eyes were on the horizon, but Darcy reckoned she did not see a thing of the beauty before them. She was puzzling out some mystery, he guessed, by the slight crease of a frown in her forehead, and the way her lips were drawn into a tight line.

"I wager you were correct in your earlier assertion," he said, after a moment's silent progress.

"I'm sorry?" Elizabeth jerked her head up.

"I startled you: forgive me." Darcy's lips quirked. "But at least this time, without the involvement of tea your dress is no casualty."

Elizabeth's frown deepened, and then relaxed. She laughed, but it was not the sound Darcy was used to. This was forced, a strange and strangled sound he did not very much care for. Nor did he care for the mood that must have caused it.

"You seem preoccupied, Miss Elizabeth. I hope you are not unwell."

"No, no." Elizabeth sighed. "I am quite well, Mr Darcy. Although I must congratulate you on your powers of observation." This was murmured with hardly any intonation, and Darcy wondered if she was even aware she had spoken the thought aloud.

"Come, come, Miss Elizabeth," he cajoled, attempting to win back a fraction of the easy style of conversation they had adopted of late. It was an unusual prospect for him, for most often it had been she, rather than he, leading the verbal dance, and he was not entirely sure of his prowess in this new role. "You value perception in your friends, do you not? Surely you wish to know what I have most recently witnessed."

"It is evident that you wish to tell me," Elizabeth muttered, but at length, she lifted her eyes to his and smiled, so he felt that all was not lost. "Please continue."

"My cousin appears utterly smitten. I wager he will wish to see your father before the week is out, if not sooner." A thought struck Darcy. "In fact, he may even enquire of Mr Bennet this very afternoon. However, my powers of understanding do not extend so strongly to your sister. I believe she cares for him, or may learn to, what say you?"

"I am surprised to see you take such an interest in affairs of the heart, Mr Darcy," Elizabeth said, glancing towards Colonel Fitzwilliam and Mary, all the same, and allowing, with the tilt of her head, that she agreed with Darcy's assessment. "Is this a new hobby of yours? *Mr Fitzwilliam Darcy, matchmaker*?"

Darcy laughed at that.

"I cannot think of a mode of employment I am less suited to. No, my caring is solely for my cousin."

"You maintain indifference to your own future?" Elizabeth sighed.

"Indifference? Hardly. But I am not - have never been - a romantic."

This provoked still another sigh, and Darcy turned with concern towards her.

"You cannot say this surprises you, Miss Elizabeth? Of all the accusations you have levied at me in our short acquaintance, I do not recall "romantic" ever being among them."

"No, no. I am merely resigned to the fact that perhaps you are right to remain always pragmatic on matters of the heart. Or perhaps that should be matters of the pocketbook."

Her eyebrows drew together once more, and Darcy felt a strange urge to reach out and smooth the lines that formed on her high forehead. Instead, he waited patiently for her to continue, sensing, somehow, that she wished to and would, given time. His patience was rewarded a moment later, when she spoke once more.

"I am sure you are well aware of the question posed to me by my cousin Mr Collins last evening." Elizabeth's cheeks coloured with embarrassment. "I am quite sure by now that half of Meryton knows, for Miss Bingley will take great delight in telling the story wherever she goes."

"She has gone nowhere today, I assure you."

Instead of having the soothing effect he had hoped for, this comment merely made Elizabeth's features fall still further.

"It is of little matter whether she tells people today or tomorrow or a week from now. It seems my fate is sealed."

"Miss Elizabeth," Darcy began. "I know little of women, although I do have a sister. I am not familiar with marriage, never yet having posed such a question as Mr Collins did to any lady of my acquaintance...thus far." He hesitated, sure of his sentiment but unsure how to best express it. He was gratified when she lifted her eyes to his and showed by attention that she listened. "But I do know this: it is a question with more than one answer. Simply because it is asked, does not mean that the answer must be yes."

To his surprise, Elizabeth laughed, the same hollow, bitter sound he had heard just a few moments before, and he berated himself for choosing his words poorly.

"Mr Darcy," Elizabeth said, with a sad smile. "If you think that, you do not know my mother."

Chapter Sixteen

Mary did not know when she had enjoyed a walk more. She certainly did not recall the journey between Meryton and Longbourn ever passing so quickly, and it was not without disappointment that they drew within view of home.

"Miss Mary," Colonel Fitzwilliam asked, as he, too, recognised the shadow of Longbourn ahead of them. "I must ask you something. It is, I am quite sure, absolutely the wrong time, and I am certain to use the wrong words and utterly mangle the telling, still, I feel that "he who hesitates is lost", and so I shall not hesitate any longer."

He frowned in concentration, and in a flash, Mary saw the image of the young boy Richard, who had got into so many scrapes with his wealthier, wiser cousin. He also seemed nervous, something Mary had never imagined him capable of being. Where was the confident, cheerful Colonel Fitzwilliam she had been speaking to moments before?

"Is everything alright?" she asked, anxious of what he was about to say. "Have I - have I done something wrong?" She ran back over her conduct that morning, and further still, to the dinner at Netherfield and dancing, to their very first meeting at Longbourn. She could not identify any action that had been out of place, yet she was so unused to spending time with gentlemen, particularly those as well travelled or worldly as the Colonel that she was sure the fault must be hers.

"You have done nothing wrong!" Colonel Fitzwilliam said, with surprise. "What on earth might you have done that was wrong? No, my dear Miss - and yet, I wish, if I may, to dispense with your title for the briefest of moments. It is too important a question to be posed as if we were strangers still. For we not strangers, are we, Mary?"

Mary felt a flood of warmth to hear her name on his lips without the precursor "Miss", and smiled, cautiously wondering what was to follow.

"Then I might speak, even though I am sure it is too soon and too sudden and I shall regret it intensely." He hesitated, then shook off whatever thought had stilled him. "No, I shall regret it more if I do not speak. For whilst I do not leave today, I shall leave soon, and I do so wish to have spoken of this before I do."

"Then speak!" Mary said, with a gentle laugh that she hoped was encouraging. She was nervous to see him to ill-at-ease, and wished to know what had so unsettled him.

"I speak of - of marriage, Miss Mary." He paused. "You see, there a title has snuck in once more, for it is a formal request, I suppose, and must be spoken of as such." He took a deep breath. "Miss Mary Bennet, I have known you but a few days, and yet it feels as if I have known you my whole life. It is as if I conjured the whole of Longbourn and you at your piano that very first day I arrived, for I stumbled upon it like a man upon a mirage. I cannot offer you a great home, or a title, or land, but I have a little fortune accrued from my career, and I think we can be happy together. I know it is too soon to hope you might care for me more than a little, but that little is all I ask. Will you marry me, Mary?"

He might just as well have spoken the words in French, or Greek, or Ancient Egyptian, for all the sense Mary made of them at first.

"You wish to-" she murmured.

"I wish to marry you, Miss Mary. If you will have me."

Mary glanced around them, to ensure they were far enough away from her sisters that they had not been overheard. Elizabeth and Mr Darcy walked together, and Jane and Mr Bingley had gone on ahead at such a pace that they had left some distance between them.

"You do not wish it."

Colonel Fitzwilliam spoke in despair as if it were fact, not a question.

"Forgive me," he continued. "I ought not to have spoken without being sure of your affections. I ought not to have spoken at all. It was too soon, too sudden -"

"Colonel Fitzwilliam," Mary said, finding her voice at last.

"Richard," he corrected her. "I think we might risk using first names just presently.

"Richard," Mary whispered, shyly. She felt strange to be using his Christian name, and yet once she uttered it she could not imagine ever calling him by another.

"You cannot truly mean to propose to me, that you wish to marry...me?"

"What other Mary would I address?" His tone was anxious, still, but there was a hint of his old teasing.

"But you cannot mean *me,*" Mary protested. "I am...nobody. Nothing."

"You are the sweetest creature I have ever met," Richard countered. "Kind, and gentle, and precisely the lady I wish to marry. Can you not see our modest little cottage, filled with music - for we shall acquire you a piano. A brand new one, one for every room if you wish it." He grinned. "And now you see the necessity of a cottage, with but a few rooms. For what little wealth I have shall otherwise go entirely on music."

"You are being ridiculous," Mary said.

"Indeed I am. Ridiculous and nonsensical and utterly serious about my feelings for *you*, Miss Mary Bennet."

He reached for her hand and Mary was surprised by how gently he held it in his. "You have not yet answered me."

"Haven't I?" Mary was honestly surprised, but when she realised she had not yet uttered the one word that would set Richard's heart at rest, she could not resist holding him in suspense a moment or two longer. "Well, now, I am not sure..."

His features had barely had time to fall before she recanted her intent, and nodded, fervently. "Yes, Colonel Fitzwilliam. I would be delighted to marry you."

"MAMA!"

Jane raised the cry as the party reached Longbourn. Lizzy haunted Mary's side, still unsure of what reception she might receive from her mother but also so happy to see her sister happy that she did not wish to let either Mary or Colonel Fitzwilliam out of her sight, lest anything change.

"She has taken herself to bed, dear cousin Jane." Mr Collins' voice rose from the parlour, and Jane and Lizzy exchanged a glance.

"You had better go, Jane. If she sees me there's likely to be still more upset and she'll think I am creating this marriage merely for sport!" Lizzy pulled Mary tight to her. "As if I would do such a thing: as if I could have imagined doing such a thing, had it not happened before my own eyes." She glanced around. "Where is Colonel Fitzwilliam?"

But the Colonel had his own plan, and had knocked smartly on Mr Bennet's study door. From within, Lizzy heard her father's weary voice calling "Come", and taking one last fortifying breath, he pushed the door open and entered. Lizzy had just time to hear Mr Bennet's warm "Why, Colonel Fitzwilliam! How pleased I am to see you!" before the door was closed.

"I wonder if I ought to have accompanied him," Mary wondered, chewing her lower lip.

"I would not worry about it, Mary. They will ask for you when they want to see you, I am sure. Besides, you cannot leave me alone with Mr Collins!" Lizzy shuddered, but as if that gentleman had heard his name and considered it a summons, he appeared in the doorway of the parlour.

"Miss Elizabeth! Miss Mary, what has happened? Did I hear Colonel Fitzwilliam's voice? What of your other guests? Pray, do invite them in, for I would dearly like to see Mr Darcy again before my departure for Kent."

"Oh, Mr Collins, are you leaving us?" Lizzy asked, her voice trilling with hope and relief.

"Well, yes -" Mr Collins began, sending her a strange look. "We -"

He was not given time to finish his sentence, for there was a great shriek from above, and Mrs Bennet's footsteps sounded heavily on the stairs.

"Mary! Mary, my dear, sweet Mary! Where are you?"

Mary scarcely had time to respond before a whirlwind, disguised as Mrs Bennet, engulfed her fully in an embrace. "You must tell me everything, dear. How did you manage to secure such a man as Colonel Fitzwilliam? Of course, I would not be content with a mere Colonel for Jane, but for any other of my daughters, such a match is to be rejoiced over." She sniffed at Elizabeth. "In fact, I congratulate you for achieving what your elder sister could not. Where is the dear man?"

"He is speaking with Father," Mary said, her voice muffled by her mother's tight embrace.

"Come, come, let us sit in the parlour and you might tell me everything! Do you know, I had a suspicion of his affection for you, but did not wish to speak, lest I spoiled everything." She laughed. "I knew, given time, he would see your sweet character and be unable to resist. Now, tell me, do you intend to marry here? And Colonel Fitzwilliam will be seeking a home, of course. I hope he will consider securing one in Hertfordshire, so that you might be around family - for I should miss you so, so much if you were wrenched away from us, Mary dear!"

Elizabeth rolled her eyes skywards, certain that Mary had never yet received so much attention from her mother as she did at this moment. In fact, Mrs Bennet largely overlooked her middle daughter, little caring whether she was at home at all, provided she was not under her feet.

"We have not decided yet," Mary said, glancing anxiously towards the parlour door, as if looking for Colonel Fitzwilliam.

"Yes, give them a moment, Mama. Father has not yet given his consent to the match. Colonel Fitzwilliam is speaking to him now."

"Well, that is merely a formality." Mrs Bennet tossed her head, shooting Elizabeth an angry look before turning pointedly back to Mary. "*He* understands the importance of duty."

What was that supposed to mean? Elizabeth could not help but return to Charlotte's words, and, almost by reflex, her eyes sought out Mr Collins who happened, at that moment, to be openly staring at her with what he evidently intended to be a mournful gaze. Unfortunately, it struck Elizabeth as comical, and she looked away quickly, before her laughter betrayed her.

"Jane, dear, I hope your Mr Bingley was witness to this happy proposal!" Mrs Bennet said, exalting over the two of her daughters who had made her most happy and ignoring the one she despaired of. "Perhaps it will encourage him to do likewise!"

"I am sure Mr Bingley will speak when the time is right," Jane said, with a shy smile. "And in any case, Mama, he and Mr Darcy are waiting just outside, so you must guard your tongue."

"I must do no such thing! Outside? Why do they wait outside?" She bustled to her feet. "Mr Bingley! You must come in at once and take tea with us, while my husband and Colonel Fitzwilliam see to their business. Oh, and you too, Mr Darcy.

Our cousin Mr Collins will be delighted for the opportunity to speak to you once more."

A masculine muttering reached the parlour but Elizabeth took it for assent, for after a moment or two more, both Mr Bingley and Mr Darcy were awkwardly thrust through the doorway to join them.

"Mr Darcy!" Mr Collins leapt to his feet, affecting a deep bow which was far too formal for so small a setting, and served only to make him look still more ridiculous than usual. Mr Darcy lifted his eyes to Elizabeth with a grimace, and again she was forced to look away to keep from laughing out loud.

"You see, Mr Bingley! But one week's acquaintance and already Colonel Fitzwilliam is conscious of his wants and wishes. That we might all make our decisions so firmly!"

"Yes, indeed, Mrs Bennet!" Mr Bigley laughed, little realising Mrs Bennet's intention was to urge him to do likewise.

The door to Mr Bennet's study opened with a flourish, and both gentlemen within came to join the rest of the party crammed into the Longbourn parlour.

"Well, my dear," Mr Bennet said, patting Colonel Fitzwilliam warmly on the shoulder. "It appears our middle daughter has outwitted us both and made a solid, dependable match, with nary a moment's interference from either parent." His eyes darkened. "If only the others might be permitted to do the same."

"All is settled?"

In this instance, both Elizabeth and her mother shared an expression of breathless anticipation. With a fervent, happy nod, Colonel Fitzwilliam set them at ease.

"All is settled. Of course, there are still a lot of arrangements to be made." He laughed. "Like securing a house, for I cannot ask my Mary to join me in outstaying my welcome at Netherfield." He beamed at his friends, but his smile faltered a fraction. "And I must keep my pledge to visit my aunt at Rosings. I wonder, Mary, if you might accompany me, for I would like her to know you, and then you might meet my cousin Anne, of whom we were speaking just today. She would love you, I know, and be a kind friend to you."

Mary hesitated.

"You may bring someone with you of course, for propriety - any one of your sisters, or all of them, for there are rooms a-plenty in Rosings."

"Oh, indeed!" Mr Collins breathed. "And I can vouch for their style, their elegance, their -"

"Did someone suggest we might take tea?" Mr Darcy said, in a vaguely irritable tone of voice, evidently desiring more to silence Mr Collins than to seek refreshment.

"Elizabeth must go with you," Mrs Bennet said, with a decided nod, quite ignoring Mr Darcy. "For that will coincide very neatly with your plans, will not it, Mr Collins?"

"Indeed!" He launched forward, securing Elizabeth's hand almost before she realised what he was doing. "Your father has consented, my dear cousin Elizabeth, and so we might marry without delay. Three weeks in Kent is all we require!"

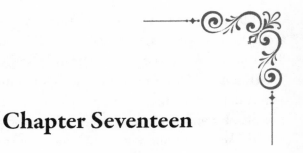

Chapter Seventeen

"It is some joke, surely? Some scheme Mama has devised to teach me a lesson. She cannot possibly mean to go through with it?"

When the truth of the situation had dawned on Elizabeth she had bid their guests farewell and made a hasty retreat to her room. Jane and Mary were forced, out of politeness and a desire, on Mary's part, to bid her newly affianced a proper goodbye, to delay following her for a few minutes, and when they, at last, reached Elizabeth's room the door had been barricaded closed. It took persuasion, and a promise that they were alone, for Elizabeth to relent and permit them to enter.

"It cannot be true?" Lizzy lifted her face from the pillow it had been buried in and turned first to Jane and then to Mary, who could do nothing but nod, sadly.

"Mama and Mr Collins must have persuaded Father while we were out," Jane said. "He never would have consented without some argument on their part."

"They wish you to be happy," Mary said quietly. "And to be well provided for. I do not think it is malicious."

"And yet they condemn me to misery my whole life!" Elizabeth burst into tears with such ferocity that Mary was shocked. She had never seen Elizabeth exhibit such emotion, and wished she could think of some way to help her sister.

"And so I must go to Kent and be paraded around as Mr Collins' bride." Lizzy shuddered. "Do you know, I actually thought I had misjudged the man, acted too hastily in refusing him. Charlotte accused me of being selfish, but now I think it is Mama being selfish, and Mr Collins too. They do not care for my feelings, only that I am married and Longbourn is safe for the future."

"You must come to Kent," Mary agreed, her mind racing. "But you need not come as Mr Collins' bride. Why not stay at Rosings with me as *my* guest? Colonel Fitzwilliam has declared I might have one - and I cannot think of a better friend in these days than you, Lizzy."

Lizzy stopped sniffling long enough to process this idea.

"You will help me think of a way out of this, Mary?"

"Yes." Mary nodded, stoutly. "Or make it a more palatable option at least. We do not know Mr Collins well, perhaps he is a perfectly fine gentleman -"

Lizzy snorted.

"Or perhaps he is a dreadful human being who I am to be shackled to for all eternity, courtesy of Mama's scheming."

"He may not be the only gentleman at Rosings," Jane mused. "Recall, Colonel Fitzwilliam has another cousin he might persuade to return with him."

"So I must endure Mr Darcy's displeasure as well as Mr Collins' preening?" Lizzy fell back on the bed in despair. "I believe you are marrying the only decent man in all of England, Mary." She eyed Jane. "Although I credit you that Mr Bingley is quite lovely and I have no doubt of you marrying him before the year is out. At least two of my sisters will be content in their matches, if I must be miserable."

Jane's eyes met Mary's over Elizabeth's head.

"We will leave you to rest, dear. This has been a very trying episode. Do not worry too much. All is not lost yet!"

As soon as the door was closed behind them, Jane reached for Mary's arm.

"I have a possible solution, but it will not work without some assistance. If you succeed in getting Lizzy to Rosings, there is half a chance, if Mr Darcy goes too..."

Mary tilted her head to one side.

"You cannot mean Lizzy and...Mr Darcy?"

"Surely you have seen them together? She comes alive with someone to argue with, and he at least can hold his own, better than any other gentleman I have known. Might they not learn to be happy together - happier, at least, than poor Lizzy and Mr Collins?"

"Does she love him?"

Jane frowned.

"That, I do not know. I fancy of the two his feelings are stronger, but Lizzy might see the advantage in choosing to be happy with Mr Darcy rather than enduring a life with Mr Collins. And love may grow over time..." She nodded. "I think it is the best we can offer. Will you try, Mary?"

"I CALL IT A JOLLY GOOD show!" Mr Bingley saluted Richard with his brandy glass. "I very much approve of marriage, and think you and Miss Mary will make a delightfully happy couple."

Richard laughed, and returned the toast with his own glass.

"You *approve of marriage?* Charles, you are practically wed already, although poor Miss Bennet must be wearily wondering if you will ever ask her."

"Do you think so?" Anxiety flickered across Bingley's face. "Oh...I had better ask her then. And soon." He smiled, a little placated. "I will discuss it with Caroline tomorrow, for she is fond of Miss Bennet too and I am sure she will be eager to help me win her hand."

Richard turned to Darcy, who was sitting in a chair in one corner of Bingley's study and nursing his drink in moody silence. His heart sank. In spite of his own happiness, he could see his cousin was devastated by the news that Elizabeth would marry Mr Collins, although he had not said a word about it. Richard wished he had, so that he could encourage him somehow that Elizabeth's own feelings were apparent in her distress at the development. She clearly did not care for Collins and had refused him once already. Richard very much doubted the marriage would ever take place, for, in spite of Mrs Bennet's enthusiasm for the match he felt certain Elizabeth's father was less enamoured. He had given his consent, indeed, but it was likely under duress and certainly not without reservation. Richard recalled the way Mr Bennet had taken his hand, congratulating him on his choice and welcoming him almost as a son. *"If only each of my daughters might make such an easy match!"* he had said, with a sad smile. It was only now that Richard understood to what he had been referring.

"I suppose I must continue with my arrangements to visit Rosings," Richard remarked, taking a burning sip of his drink. "There is little cause for delay, now that my main concern is settled, and I do so wish for Mary and Anne to meet." He risked a second glance at his cousin. "I even think Aunt Catherine might find it in her heart to be happy for me."

"Perhaps." Darcy lifted his glance, at length.

"You are welcome to join me, cousin," Richard pressed, after a long moment's silence. He turned to Bingley. "Not that I wish to deprive you of all your guests at once."

"Not at all!" Charles grinned. "You may do precisely as you please, both of you, and know that you are welcome to return to Netherfield whenever you wish to."

"Darcy." Richard leant forward, leaning his elbows on his knees and facing his cousin directly. "I am going to speak freely, and say what I ought to have said when I first arrived. You may rage against me, but I have known you long enough to withstand your fury. And in any case, 'tis a day of renown for me, and you must permit me a little leeway in my behaviour, today of all days. If you care for Elizabeth Bennet, you must speak, and speak now. She is not married yet."

Darcy frowned, but Richard could not quite discern whether his reaction was down to a bitter disappointment at the state of affairs between Elizabeth and Mr Collins, or a profound irritation that Richard had so correctly guessed his feelings.

"It was plain to all present, except perhaps to Mr Collins and Mrs Bennet, who are both so focused on their own desires, that Elizabeth does not wish to marry him. I rather think she might accept any alternative offered to her." He let his voice rest forcefully on the words "any alternative" in hopes his meaning might be plain to Darcy. His cousin was of a pragmatic bent, and would surely see that although any offer of marriage he made to Elizabeth Bennet now could not hope to be a romantic one, it could at least be a practical opportunity for escape that she would likely grab at with both hands. They would learn to love each other, or learn to acknowledge the fact that they already did, that much Richard was sure of, if only they could preserve the opportunity to learn it. If that meant marriage, Richard would support it. He cared for his cousin and wished his happiness. And, through Mary, he cared for Elizabeth too. As a gentleman, he disliked the thought of any woman being pressed into a match she despised, on the whims of those who professed an interest in her future. The Bennets were not wealthy, but they were surely not impoverished enough that such a sacrifice was necessary?

"Come to Rosings with me," Richard said, impetuously. "I shall need you on my side to tackle Aunt Catherine, and I do not doubt Mary and Elizabeth will be eager for your companionship as well."

Darcy's brows lowered further still, but Richard would not be put off.

"Three weeks is all I ask, for look at all that has taken place in just a few days! Who knows what three weeks may yield?"

The End

About the Author

Meg Osborne[1] is an avid reader, tea drinker and unrepentant history nerd. She writes sweet historical romance stories and Jane Austen fanfiction, and can usually be found knitting, dreaming up new stories, or adding more books to her tbr list than she'll get through in a lifetime.

For updates and new release news – and early access to whatever stories Meg is currently working on, follow her on Ream[2]!

---

1. https://reamstories.com/megosbornewrites

2. https://reamstories.com/megosbornewrites

Printed in the USA
CPSIA information can be obtained
at www.ICGtesting.com
LVHW041605200424
777982LV00004B/630